NIGHTMARE'S FALL

Dreambound
Book Two

By
Dakota Brown

Nightmare's Fall
A Reverse Harem Tale

Dreambound, Book 2

Inkwolf Press
P.O. Box 473
Ault, Colorado
80610

ISBN: 979-8-9864144-1-6

www.inkwolfpress.com

PRODUCED IN THE UNITED STATES OF AMERICA

10 9 8 7 6 5 4 3 2 1

DEDICATION

To Chrissa:
Thank you for introducing me to the pain hoop, aka Lyra. I
love every minute of it.

ACKNOWLEDGEMENTS

I want to throw a special shout out to the circus center where I train, and the instructors who make my time there so special. I couldn't have written this book without the knowledge and skills I've gained there. The community is so supportive and I love you all.

A huge thank you to my editors, Rachelle Hobbs and Aeryn Havens. Thank you SO much for all your insights. Make sure you read their books!

Thank you to my proofing team. Obviously any remaining mistakes are mine.

I want to shout out a special thank you for my patrons on Patreon: Melynda, Yashira, Jacqui, Kori, Shay, Caitlin, Vivian, Margaret, Teri, Rachel, Michael, Jacqulin, Paula, and V. Kittie. Thank you for your extra support.

And last, but certainly the most important, thank you, Readers, for picking up my book and devouring it, then asking for more.

CHAPTER 1

Ember

Air rushed past me, and adrenalin sent my heart racing as I fell backward. *Shit, shit... no, it's all right.* I came up hard against the silks wrapped around my legs, spinning at the bottom of my drop, and my panic quieted at that comforting pressure. I let my momentum change my path and flip me upright. Arms outstretched and toes pointed, I ended the move. Remembering that all important smile, I posed before untangling myself and climbing to the ground.

A handful of captivated teens clapped.

Conscious of the group of parents that observed their children training, I didn't give voice to the relief I felt at not having a panic attack after the drop. It was a relatively simple one. However, it wasn't but a few days ago that climbing the silks without freaking out was beyond me. Where once I'd soared with complete confidence, fake-Baz's cruel games in Nightmare had broken that. Knowing Nic lurked in the shadows, unseen though I could feel his presence, and my budding powers gave me a little more confidence. He'd catch me if the silks vanished, and I failed to catch myself.

"Sadie, you try it." I wiped the sweat from my brow.

The teen grinned and ran over to the set of silks I had just used.

1

"Use a dancer climb," I ordered. There were a ton of different ways to climb up the silks, and this was a pretty basic one, but it wasn't the easiest—though it was far from truly difficult—and I wanted her to work a little.

She pushed her lips out in a fake pout before wrapping her leg around the fabric and starting her climb. I watched while she set herself up for the drop, talking her through a few points since she'd never done it before. When she let go, a huge grin on her face as she flew through the air, I remembered my first time. I'd been young and fearless, but I'd still had a moment's pause to think about how I was about to fling myself toward the ground from fifteen feet in the air. The rush of a first successful plunge in the silks had stuck with me all these years and I still loved it, despite my current fears.

If I got the chance, I was going to punch not-Baz in the fucking face for putting uncertainty in my life. Well, maybe I'd use a big stick. I'd never punched anyone in my life, and I suspected I might hurt myself. The pain might be worth it, though.

Tonight, Geraint and I were going to try one of our warmup straps routines. If that went well, we'd work back up to our full sequences. He and I both had a little catching up to do after several weeks of very little aerial. Even knights of the realm of Nightmare had to keep in shape.

Of course, I hadn't known Geraint was a being from Nightmare sent to keep me safe after a childhood game of "wedding" had bound me to three Nightmare princes. Geraint and I had grown up together, fallen in love, created the perfect life touring the world with our renowned performances.

Then someone imitating one of my princes had decided he wanted me back in Nightmare. It took not-Baz a while to find me, but when he had, he'd kidnapped both me and Geraint, tortured us, and locked us away. One of the castle guards more loyal to the realm than to Baz himself had helped Geraint arrange my escape, and I'd found Nic. Prince Nyctophobia, the embodiment of the fear of the dark or the unknown. He had these kick-ass shadow powers, and he was actually just as nice as I remembered from our play as children. Meeting him had unlocked all those magically sealed memories and turned my world upside down.

Now we were trying to balance a semblance of a normal life while Nic hid out in the conscious realm with me and Geraint, while also trying to figure out what had happened to Prince Dio and the real Prince Baz.

I'd accepted my role as the princess of Nightmare, but I didn't really know what that meant yet. Other than mind blowing sex with Nic, and Geraint, and slowly developing my own shadow powers.

"Great job, dancers," I said as the last of my students finished their practice. "Cool down, and I'll see you next time!" Some of them would be back tomorrow, some only came weekly.

Geraint worked with another group on the other side of the gym. They were training with straps. I stared after my knight wistfully before tearing my gaze away. Done teaching for the day, I wanted to get food before practice with my knight later.

Late afternoon humidity slapped me in the face when I stepped outside of the air-conditioned gym. I wiped at my face and headed for the flower gardens that bordered the pathway to the house. Flies buzzed in the still air. I hurried for the big shade tree, an invisible pull drawing me toward it.

Prince Nic sat at the base of the tree, staring out at the riot of color the flowers presented. A flock of hand-raised geese wandered through our flowers, picking at the weeds and generally helping us keep up with the place. It was

3

easier to hose goose poop off the walk than it was to weed the gardens. A chicken darted past, chasing a bug, and I knew our guardian dogs wouldn't be far. Inhaling the perfume of all the blooms and wishing I had my sketch book, I grinned and sank down onto the ground next to Nic. I'd grab food in a minute.

"Hey." I bumped my shoulder against his.

"Hello, Ember." He folded his hand around mine and squeezed.

"How are you holding up?"

Nic grinned. "I enjoy the conscious realm. I enjoy your company, and I'm growing used to your knight. If it weren't for the rest, it would be an extremely pleasant vacation."

That Nic wasn't hating life hanging out with me and Knight at my parents' home made my heart swell a little.

"I'm also enjoying lurking in the shadows and *spying* on you while you teach your classes or practice." He winked at me before turning his attention back out to whatever he'd been watching in the distance.

I looked but didn't see anything.

"Use your awareness of the shadows. See if you can look through them."

Frowning, I did what Nic said. The heat from the day faded from my awareness, bringing me into the velvety cool darkness of the shadows. Every day, my connection to these powers grew stronger, but my control was still tenuous at best.

"I feel them," I said. "I can see blackness. That's it."

He squeezed my hand again. "It'll come. Robby somehow snuck back through the arch in the cabin. He's on his way. Some Nightmare hounds are sniffing around, but they won't last long in the conscious realm."

"Thanks." Trying not to get frustrated at my lack of ability with the shadows, I slid my hand from Nic's and climbed to my feet. "I'll grab some food and meet you both back out here. Even if Robby isn't hungry, I am."

"I'll see you in a bit," Nic said as I left.

"Hey, Ember," Casey, my friend from the performance contract in the spring, called as I hurried to the house. She'd taken me up on my offer for a summer position teaching at my parents' camp.

"Yeah?" I waited for her to catch up.

"I was just heading to the kitchen. You?"

I nodded and waited, despite the heat, until she reached my side. We walked together without talking and I got the impression Casey was working up toward asking me what she thought might be an awkward question. If so, it likely either had to do with my recent issues with the silks, or Nic. Neither of which I had a suitable answer for. I was seriously tempted to tell her the truth and see what she made of it.

"Have you seen Robby recently?" she finally asked.

That was not what I'd expected, and it took me a moment to reply. "He's been looking into some things, but I think he'll be back soon."

"He's single, right?"

Oh. I almost warned her off, but then reconsidered. The Dream court jester drove me nuts, but he was considerate, and would understand her obsession with her lyra.

"Yes, Casey, he's single. He's been single as long as I've known him."

"Great. Put in a good word for me?" She widened her eyes and shot me a hopeful expression.

Laughing, I nodded. "Okay, Casey. Did you ever get in touch with him about that winter gig?"

"Oh, yeah, I sent him an email about it. He said you all were interested, and he'd look into it."

"Perfect." I had no idea if we'd be able to commit to anything this winter, but I didn't want to give up my career completely if I could avoid it.

"So who's Nic?"

That was the question I was expecting. "Childhood friend."

"You two seem awfully close whenever I actually see him. What's he doing here?"

"Hanging out for the summer. He's a friend of Robby's and Geraint's, too. And yes, we're close."

"Geraint—"

"Nic and I were close before Geraint and I were close. We both thought Nic was gone for good, through no fault of his own. Now that Nic is back, we're reworking our relationship to include Nic. It's best for everyone that way." It wasn't necessarily any of her business, but it was also easier just to tell her.

"You sure?" She shook her head. "I'm sorry. It's probably not my business. Non-traditional relationships work out all the time. I just know how crazy Geraint is about you and—"

"Yeah. We're sure." I opened the door to the house and hurried into the cool air.

"Well, damn then, two men who are crazy about you. Lucky you. Does Nic perform too?"

"No. But he'll be fantastic stage crew."

We went through the den with the big mirror that I'd once crashed through with Nic in tow, escaping Nightmare. A couple of our campers were watching TV when we went through to the kitchen.

Our summer chef, Larry, was cutting food for dinner in the industrial-sized kitchen. He paused long enough to point at the refrigerator. "Sandwiches inside, ladies."

Larry had a thick Appalachian accent that evoked fond memories of my childhood. Growing up here in the foothills of the Allegheny mountains brought us a whole mix of people, and some of the folks who lived in the mountains brought their kids down to the summer camp.

"Thanks!" We helped ourselves and went out onto the screened back porch.

Fans circulated the air, making the heat a bit more tolerable. I downed some water and scarfed my sandwich.

"Speaking of," Casey said, looking over my shoulder back toward the house.

I twisted around. Nic and Robby came out onto the porch, heading our way. Robby held a sandwich and a glass of water. *Oh, right. I was supposed to meet them back in the garden.* Casey had distracted me.

"Robby!" I jumped to my feet and threw my arms around him. He managed not to spill the water on me, or drop his sandwich. Nic took them from the jester so he could hug me properly.

"You're not dead!" I blurted, forgetting Casey was there for a moment.

"No, princess, I'm quite alive." He retrieved his plate from Nic and sat next to Casey at the table.

Her eyes widened, and she looked down at her plate.

Robby didn't act like he noticed, but he probably did. The jester was, by his very nature, highly observant. It made him a fantastic manager for my aerial business.

Nic sat next to me, and I touched my leg to his under the table. My shadowy prince was making an effort to remain fully solid since we were around others. Normally, he shifted in and out of shadow. Sunlight was hard on him, too. Fading him out to flat shades of gray unless he put forth the energy to look human. Some of his features shifted with his mood. He currently had his black hair longer, and tied back in a tail. High cheekbones and tawny skin accented his angular eyes and handsome features. Nic was a prince of Nightmare, but he spoke with a light Kiwi accent I loved.

Casey studied Robby, probably wondering why I'd been amazed he was alive. I could understand why she liked him. The jester had wavy brown hair that looked soft and very pettable. His brown eyes were gentle with laugh lines at his temples and his neatly trimmed beard and goatee didn't hurt his appearance any. Robby was taller than Geraint, but not nearly as tall as Nic, and both men were leaner than my knight by a fair bit.

I was dying to ask him what news he had, and his eyes twinkled mischievously. I hoped that his light mood meant the news wasn't terrible. Of course, with him, it could be, and he was simply amused at making me wait.

"Casey," he said, voice almost too smooth. "How are you enjoying summer camp?"

She swallowed, visibly gathering herself. I hid my amusement by taking a drink.

"It's good. I'm enjoying teaching the kids, and Ember's parents are every bit as fantastic as I thought they would be." She turned her smile on me.

I nodded. "They are pretty cool."

"Yeah, having a glimpse of what it's like living with supportive parents is eye opening." A sad smile flitted across Casey's lips.

Robby put his hand over Casey's. She nearly melted. He had to know she was interested, but how he'd figured it out when I'd only just learned, I didn't know. Unless Nic had been spying and relayed it. Which, considering I'd said I would meet him in the garden, and I'd ended up here instead, wasn't out of the question. *Maybe I should tell Robby not to break her heart.*

"You're an amazing talent, Casey. Don't let anyone hold you back." He fixed her with his most charming smile. It wasn't quite as good as Geraint's panty-melting one, but it was effective.

"Thanks," she stuttered.

Nic smirked. I just shook my head.

"Ember, do you have a minute?" Nic stood and held out his hand.

"Yeah. Catch up with you two later." I slid my hand into my prince's and let him help me stand. We left Robby to his flirting and went back inside.

Nic sighed in relief once we were in the darker air conditioning, and I let him drag me back toward my room, where he immediately dissolved into shadow for a few moments, before stepping out of them and sinking into the rocking chair he shared with Geraint.

"You okay?"

"Yes, of course. It's simply a relief to be out of the sunlight. The jester has news. Dio is most certainly in the conscious realm. The real Baz is still missing, but the jester has promising leads. The fake Baz is growing more unstable by the moment, and things are getting awful for everyone in Nightmare. Robby isn't sure how we will return. He just barely got out, and the Lady in White is no longer able to help him. She's not captured, but they've corrupted the arches between realms and she barely got this one to function."

"If the arches are broken, how are they getting through?"

Nic shook his head. "I wish I knew. I believe I mentioned that some powerful dreams and nightmares can simply leak through to the conscious realm. Beings with a lot of human belief behind them. They are likely the ones we have to contend with. I have no idea how Baz got the hounds through."

"Okay."

He held out his hand again, and I took it, letting me tug him into his lap. He wrapped me in his arms, coiling shadows around my waist and legs, and rested his cheek against my head.

I let him hold me, sharing my energy with him. As his princess and mate, we could help revitalize each other this way. He ran his fingers over my arm, and I snuggled into him, content to sit here for a while.

A soft knock on the door interrupted us a little while later. Geraint came in, Robby right behind. Geraint sat on the bed, and Robby leaned against the door frame.

"You've gotten cozy while I've been away." Robby mock-leered at us.

I flipped him off, then thought I should throw out a warning about Casey before we got distracted.

"Don't break her heart."

"I would never break anyone's heart, princess." Robby put his hand on his chest as if swearing.

"Somehow, I don't believe you."

He smiled. "Nic was kind enough to warn me of her confession, so you didn't have to."

That confirmed that theory. I glanced up at my Nightmare prince.

"Sorry," he murmured.

"Fine, just, don't hurt her. So, what do we need to know?"

"Dio is here. I have theories, and I will apply myself to finding him, now that I've returned. You continue playing with your men while I do all the work. I will inform you when I have something useful to share."

"I take back my excitement that you're not dead, Robby," I muttered.

He laughed. "You love me, and you know it, princess. This type of work is my specialty. Leave me to it. Though I may enlist your cousin's aid if Ash is available."

"Call her. She's been swamped with her current case lately."

"I'll do that. Geraint said you had a show coming up?"

"It's just a local charity thing for the school. Same stuff we normally do in the summer. We're going to practice tonight, make sure I can handle it."

"You'll stun them all, princess." He bowed slightly and let himself out of our room, leaving me alone with Geraint and Nic.

The two of them were getting along all right. Our arrangement was easier for Geraint to accept than Nic, since he'd always assumed he'd lose me at some point, anyway. He was thrilled he got to keep me. Nic was not completely happy with Geraint's and my involvement, but as I'd said many times, it was my body and my choice who I loved. He'd accepted that. Hopefully, my other two princes would, too. If I ever found them. Nightmare's survival depended on it, so I hoped Robby could work his magic yet again.

We sat in uncomfortable silence for a bit before Geraint shifted and cleared his throat. "We have about a half an hour until the gym is clear for us to practice."

"That sounds great, Geraint."

Nic kissed my neck, and for a moment I thought he was making some sort of claim in front of Geraint, but then he released his hold on me. "You two should probably discuss your performance."

I shifted off his lap, and he stood. "I'll be out in the woods. I'm going to look around and see if I can figure out how he got the hounds through."

"Be careful, your highness," Geraint said. "I'm supposed to be protecting you."

Nic smiled. "You're supposed to be protecting our princess. Take care of her. I'll stick to the shadows." Nic stepped backward into one of the heavier shadows in our room—we kept the curtains drawn for his comfort most of the time—and melted away.

"That's such a cool trick," I said.

Geraint took me in his arms. "You will be able to do it, too, one of these days." His familiar Irish lilt soothed me.

"Maybe," I grumbled. "I'm not getting very good at any of them except manipulating the shadow stuff into different styles of clothing."

"It is possible that it's because you're in the conscious realm instead of Nightmare," he pointed out. "You might have an easier time learning your new skills there."

I sighed. "Maybe. But it sounds like we're stuck here for the time being." I snuggled against his firm chest and rested there. Not long ago, I'd wondered if I'd ever see my knight again. There was still danger, but at least I knew what was going on now.

Geraint pressed his lips to my temple and walked us backward until he perched on the edge of my bed, and he could pull me into his lap.

"We have half an hour," he said innocently. "What do you want to do?"

I looked up at him through my eyelashes before batting them coyly. "We should probably talk about our routine. It's been months since we practiced it."

"Probably," he murmured in agreement, leaning over and nuzzling my neck. "I think I'd rather do other things."

"I'm sure you would," I replied, rapidly warming to the idea. "I think I'd rather do other things, too."

"Oh?"

"Yeah." Of course, I wasn't wearing my clothing that was created from dream essence. That stuff was super handy. I could make it flow off my body like water. I'd have to get undressed the old-fashioned way.

Geraint slipped his hands under my tank top, cupping my waist before dragging his fingers up my ribs, pulling my top up as he went.

I raised my arms in the air, and he removed the shirt. He didn't even try to be elegant when he pulled my sports bra off over my head. Long experience had led us to the conclusion that there wasn't a sexy way to remove that tight article of clothing.

"Should we do shower sex?" Geraint rumbled as he shifted me on his lap so he could pull his sweaty t-shirt off. "We're both a little fragrant."

I laughed. "I love the way your sweat smells, Knight. Let's shower after."

His eyes twinkled with amusement. "Just making sure, Spark."

We quickly finished stripping, and I pushed him onto his back. He lay there, thick cock standing at attention and ready for me. Just the thought of riding my knight had me wet. I crawled forward on my knees, straddling Geraint's legs, then I rubbed my wet pussy across his hard dick.

Geraint sucked in his breath and grabbed my hips. I rocked back and forth gently, pleasuring myself on his cock while he watched, mouth slightly open, eyes cloudy with lust.

"How did I get so lucky to be in your life?" Geraint whispered.

"You think you're the lucky one?" I replied, voice thick.

Geraint shifted one hand from my waist, tracing a line down my stomach until he could circle my clit with his thumb.

Thoughts fled as my pleasure built. Pressure built in my core, begging for release and I moaned encouragement.

Geraint obliged, stroking me until the pressure released, my juices flooding onto his twitching cock.

"Need you riding me," Geraint gasped out.

"I need that, too."

My knight grinned and lifted me until his cock pressed against my entrance. Reveling in the delicious stretch, I lowered myself until he was fully caged inside me. He kept his hands firmly on my waist and thrust with his hips, grinding into me. I cupped my breasts and played with my nipples while he rubbed me from the inside.

"Yeah, I'm definitely the lucky one," I managed to gasp out before dropping a hand to stroke my clit. Between the two of us, I was ready to fall over the edge into another orgasm just as Geraint's rhythm sped up.

"Any time, my love," I gasped.

He let himself go, and I crashed after him, collapsing into his arms as he held me against him, and we rode our endorphin highs. As I lay there, I noticed shadows curled around his legs and upper arms. Reaching out with tentative fingers, I called one of them to me.

It responded, sliding a tendril up Geraint's chest, and curling around my wrist.

"I did it!"

My knight chuckled. "Of course you did, my spark." His faith in me never wavered. "Now, shower and then you're going to dance in the sky with me."

"I love you, Geraint," I whispered.

"I love you too, Ember. I always have, and I always will."

CHAPTER 2

Ember

I love you. Three simple words, one simple phrase, yet it meant so much to hear from Geraint. He'd used the phrase sparingly our entire relationship until recently. Now I knew why, but it still made my heart swell to hear him utter those words. It felt like now that there were no more secrets between us, our relationship had moved to a new, more intense level. I stared at my lover while he dried off and marveled at the powerful muscles years of aerial work had given him.

I touched the shadows and curled them around Geraint's legs. He glanced down, then winked at me. "Show off." His wink and the pleasure in his sexy Irish lilt, let me know how proud he was of my accomplishment.

I flushed happily at his praise.

If we were alone when we got to the gym, I'd show Nic my new skills, but it might have to wait until later. Chances were my parents would be there, and I wasn't comfortable showing them any sort of powers. They weren't completely happy with my relationship with Nic, but he continued to low-key try to win them over.

Geraint reached out and caressed my cheek. "Ready, my spark?" Geraint toweled his hair dry, gray eyes shining with excitement.

"As ready as I can be," I answered.

My knight dropped his towel and came over to stand in front of me. He put his hands on my shoulders and kissed my forehead. "Spark, you will be perfect, and I'll never drop you. Nic will be there to catch us if anything strange happens."

I took a breath and nodded. "I know, Geraint. It's just hard. I never minded jumping from heights into water, but falling has never been my favorite, and not-Baz made it that much worse."

He pulled me into his arms, and I couldn't help a slightly provocative wiggle against his bare body.

Geraint chuckled. "It'll be all right, Ember. And if at any point you need to stop, we'll just change the routine and build back up to this one."

"It's already one of our older performances."

"It's a free charity event. We'll do our absolute best for them, of course, but we don't have to push ourselves."

I nodded. "You're right. Let's go."

"Mind if I pull on some pants first? We're not putting on that kind of show."

Laughing, I pulled away and snatched his towel off the ground to hang it properly. "Put some pants on. Learn to clean up after yourself."

He ruffled my hair as he passed, as he had done when we were kids. I snapped his ass with the towel and giggled when he yelped and hurried to the bedroom.

"Maybe I won't give you that treat I got for you then," he said from the other room.

"What?" I hung the towel and joined him.

Geraint pulled a package out of his gym bag and tossed it at me. I caught it and my eyes lit up at the enticing crinkle of plastic.

"Oh, my god, I haven't had chocolate-covered expresso beans since Robby took my last ones away."

Eagerly, I opened the package and shoved one in my mouth. "Mmmm, milk chocolate. The best."

"He'll probably steal those, too, so don't let him see you with them. I think he secretly likes them."

"Robby, aerial manager, Dream court jester, expresso bean lover. Who knew?" I popped another one in my mouth before stashing the package in a drawer in my dresser. "I probably needed to cut back a little, but he didn't have to steal all of them."

Geraint squeezed my shoulder. "Okay, let's go."

Feeling like I was heading off to an actual performance complete with jitters, I followed Geraint out of our room and through the house. Heavenly aromas drifted from the kitchen. A small part of me wanted to wander that way instead and investigate what had to be some sort of savory dinner combined with a sweet dessert. That was the part of me that still trembled when I dreamed of falling during not-Baz's cruel game. The rest of me was determined to fully conquer this fresh fear. I didn't want him to have any hold over me when it finally came time to confront not-Baz.

I glanced in the mirror over the fireplace as we passed through the den, hoping for a glimpse of a nightmare visage looking back at me, but it remained blank. None of us knew what had happened to Bloody Mary after she'd helped Nic escape, but we all feared the worse. Where once in my life I'd avoided looking in mirrors after dark, now I actively sought her out. Nothing yet, but I intended to find out what had happened to her. Somehow.

There were a lot of things I intended to do at some point as the Nightmare princess, but I had no idea how I would do them and I put off thinking about it. Far better to focus on this performance with Geraint and learning my cool shadowy powers. We had to find Dio before we could do anything else, anyway. Or so I told myself.

We hurried through the warm afternoon and into the cool gym.

Geraint sighed. I glanced around his shoulder and clenched my jaw, not sure how to feel. My parents had apparently told the campers to come watch. They all sat in the bleachers, and my parents stood on the stage as if they were going to coach us. I hadn't planned on using the stage. I hadn't planned on an audience. I wasn't upset that my parents were there, however. It was always good to have someone watch us now and again.

I sensed Nic lurking in the shadows backstage, probably uncomfortable with everyone being there.

"I guess it's good practice," Geraint said with a sigh.

"To be fair, we've never minded before."

He took my hand and squeezed it before tucking my arm under his and walking with me up to the stage.

"You two take a minute to get ready," Mom said with a smile. "We'll keep them entertained for a bit."

Dad spoke with the audience before walking over to the dangling straps to demonstrate something.

"Thanks, Mom."

We headed backstage. Nic lounged in a chair, waiting for us. He stood as soon as we were close. "Good discussion?"

"Yes, very." I let him fold me into his arms for a quick hug.

Mom came back just then, but other than a quick tightening of her lips until she glanced at Geraint, she didn't react.

I pulled away and slid out of my warmups, revealing the mint green leotard I wore underneath. Geraint pulled off his shirt, and I might have drooled a little. His pants matched my leo.

"Ready?" Nic smiled kindly.

I took a breath. "Yeah. Knight?"

"Of course." Geraint handed me the rosin so we could give our hands some grip aid. Centering myself, I watched Knight. There was only him and me, and that was all that mattered.

The world fell away as he took my hand and held it up as if presenting me to the audience. The first strains of the slow rock ballad filtered from the speakers. Gazes locked together, Geraint and I went out onto the stage, walking until we were just under the dangling straps.

He gently twisted my hand, slowly spinning me until my back was to his. We sank to the ground together, hands reaching upward. Geraint caught the straps in his hands and raised himself upward until he was doing a handstand in the air. I sensuously lay back to the ground, watching as my knight playfully danced into the air above me, our routine a bit of a play on a courtship between two lovers.

If we had an older audience, I'd add some movements that would show exactly how I felt about watching Geraint in the air above me. As it was, he had all my attention as he held himself parallel to the ground over me with just the strength in his powerful arms and shoulders, core tightened to keep him in a plank position.

I licked my lips so only he could see. Geraint winked before lowering himself back to the ground next to me, landing on his knees, one arm still stretched high, caught in the straps, the other coming to take my hand and spin me around until I was on my knees.

I twisted, leaning back, and he slid his hand under my neck, raising me to my feet and cradling me with my back against his chest while his free hand slid back into the hand hold. Putting my arms out in a T shape over his biceps, I let him support my body. I pulled my knees up while he spun us around, partially suspended, though he kept one foot on the ground.

The momentum took me as I set my feet down, spinning me away for a moment, before I came back behind my knight and hooked my arms around his shoulders. He leaned forward, and I leaned back, my shoulders on his. I did a slow flip over backward until we were both suspended, him by the straps, me by my knight. We spun in a circle, counterbalanced together.

The movements were so natural, so practiced, so right, that I lost myself in them. Not thinking beyond the next counterbalance, or the signal Geraint sent me to warn me of the next shift in our weight.

He moved us until we both hung down toward the ground, and I slowly climbed him, hooking a leg over his shoulder and making my way up until I stood, all while we spun in the air.

This was where I was meant to be. Flying in Geraint's arms. My heart felt close to bursting with the joy coursing through me.

I slid my way down until he cradled me again, then brought us both to the ground. He helped me switch places, sliding my hands into the straps, then lifting me until I spun with one leg hooked over my arms, the other outstretched, back arched, and he sank to the ground, to watch my part of the courtship.

The familiar burn of muscles and the pressure of the strap on my wrist as I twisted my body into different shapes above my lover felt like coming home after too long away. I had to blink away a couple of tears as I stretched my legs into a vertical split, one leg above me wrapped around the strap, one stretched below.

Knight stood, and I lowered myself until my feet touched the ground. He took the strap, pulled me to his chest and spun us until we flew together as the rock ballad picked up intensity. I slid down his body until I lay parallel to the ground, one of his legs trapped between my thighs, the other foot cradling my neck. I put my arms out and reveled in our connection as he spun us through the air.

Knight reached down, took my hand, and we flowed through a couple more shapes together before I touched the ground again.

This time we each took a strap, mirroring each other's moves as we flew together in perfect sync, showing a courtship turned into a practiced relationship between two lovers.

As the music came to a close, we slowed our spin, lowering to the ground, releasing the straps from our grasp and sinking to the stage together.

It wasn't until then that I heard the enthusiastic clapping from our audience. I'd forgotten about them completely in our dance.

Geraint stood and pulled me to my feet. We took a quick bow, then hurried backstage.

"Well done," Nic said, voice strangely tight.

For now, I wasn't going to let whatever was on his mind bring me down from my high. I'd done it, and I hadn't had one moment of fear.

My knight pulled me into his arms, and we held each other while we got our breathing under control.

"That was amazing," I whispered.

"You were perfect, as always, Spark." He kissed my head.

I glanced over at Nic, and he had his normal neutral but friendly expression on his face, so maybe I'd imagined the tightness earlier.

"You both looked amazing," Nic said.

Geraint released me and pushed me gently toward the prince. Nic accepted, folded me into his arms, Geraint standing close behind me.

CHAPTER 3

Nic

Watching Ember and the knight from backstage was eye opening to say the least. The connection the two of them had was nothing short of supernatural. The amount of work they'd put in together astounded me. Until now, I hadn't actually understood what the knight had thought he'd be giving up. I knew they loved each other, but the depth of that connection blazed as they soared together in the air.

I questioned if I should even try to continue being involved with Ember outside of what was required to save Nightmare. Those thoughts gave me a semblance of an idea about how the knight had felt when he thought he was losing his spark.

Robby stepped from the shadows next to me in the way that jesters did. "Are you sure you don't want him dead?"

"I thought you two were friends."

"The good of the realm outweighs any friendships, and Nightmare needs a princess and its princes."

"Breaking Ember to save the dreamlands won't save anything at all," I replied.

Robby bowed his head slightly.

"Any news, jester?"

"Regarding Dio? Yes. Ash is extremely clever. I'd suspect her of being a jester were she not merely mortal.

We think he might have ended up in some sort of hospital or assisted living situation for adults with mental difficulties."

"Mental difficulties?"

"There was a case about five years back of a man matching Dio's general description breaking into a museum and trying to steal something. He was found to be mentally incompetent and locked away."

"How could you possibly have found something that quickly?" I wasn't even sure what to think about Dio having lost his mental capabilities.

"We surmised that Dio would have used a familiar arch if he were fleeing, so we concentrated our search in this area."

"So we know where he is?"

Robby shook his head. "Records are sketchy, which has positively infuriated dear Ash. We have several places to check and the name of the museum he was attempting to rob."

"Why would he want to rob a museum?"

"Why, indeed?" Robby shrugged again. "I suppose we will have to find out."

"Do you know?" With the jester, it could be anything.

"No. I don't. When is their charity event?"

"Next week."

"That gives us plenty of time to do a little investigating. Hopefully, Ember doesn't mind being pulled away from her teaching duties."

"I don't think she'll mind," I said.

The music quickened its pace, and I turned my attention back to my lover and her lover as they moved in perfect harmony together.

"They're amazing, aren't they?"

"Yes." I sighed.

Robby clapped me on the shoulder. "At least she likes you, too."

"I question if I should interfere even as much as I have." I glanced at the jester, wondering if he had the answer.

His eyes glinted dangerously. "I think for the knight's sake, you should continue as you are."

I raised my eyebrows and slipped into the shadows for a moment before solidifying again.

"Unless you want him gone."

"No, I don't."

"Then carry on as you have been, and all will be well. I will wait for you three in Ember's room. She always needs a little while to decompress after a performance before she can think about much else. We can make travel plans." Robby grinned as if he hadn't just threatened to kill Ember's knight twice and turned sideways, vanishing.

No closer to any sort of peace of mind, I watched their last movements and hoped Ember wouldn't notice my troubled thoughts.

***

"That feels so good," she murmured as I kneaded her shoulders.

We sat under the big shade tree with the drooping branches in the gardens. It was a little light for my tastes, but it was tolerable. Geraint sat cross-legged next to us. I leaned against the smooth tree trunk, and Ember sat in front of me.

"I've been doing this my entire life, and I still get sore if I take time off."

Geraint flexed his hands. "So do I."

"Oh, Nic!" Ember twisted around so she could grin at me. "I did something new."

"Yes, Princess?"

She shut her eyes, scrunching her forehead in concentration. Then the shadows came alive around us. One cold strand twined up my arm before they all dissipated.

Ember sucked in a few breaths, sweat beading on her head from the exertion before she opened her eyes and looked at me again.

I smiled, brushing my thumb along her cheekbone. "Well done, luv."

"Hello, Casey," Geraint said, warning us we were no longer alone.

Hopefully before the lyrist could see me, I forced myself completely solid.

"Hi, Geraint!" Casey said brightly. "You two are the definition of amazing." She sank down to the ground across from Ember. "Hi, Ember, Nic."

"Hello, Casey," I said.

"Hey, I didn't realize you were watching." Ember leaned back against my chest.

"And miss an opportunity to see the two of you perform? Not a chance."

Geraint leaned back on his elbows. "Ready for your act next week?"

"Yeah, totally." She grinned. "Do you know if Robby has figured out your winter plans yet?"

"I am nearly positive we're accepting the same gig you are," Geraint replied. "There are a few things still up in the air, but we should know soon enough."

"That's fantastic." Her face lit up with happiness.

Her infatuation with the jester was quite entertaining. I had no idea how Robby would handle it, but I hoped tactfully. Our conversation earlier intruded on my thoughts. I believed that he really would kill Geraint to protect the dream realms. I supposed that was part of his job, to make sure Dream had what it needed to survive.

"Do you know where he is?" Casey asked shyly.

"No, but we'll make sure he knows to look for you," I lied smoothly, running my hand gently over Ember's arm.

"Thanks, Nic." She climbed to her feet. "I've got a few things to do before dinner. See you all later."

Ember glanced up at me.

"He's waiting for us in your room," I supplied. She'd clearly sensed my lie. Our connection was deepening the more time we spent together, as it should.

"We should see what he wants," Ember said.

"We have a good idea of where Dio is," I filled her in. "We simply need to investigate."

She shot to her feet. "Let's go, then."

We stood and followed Ember back to the house. Sure enough, Robby waited in her room, snacking on something.

"Hey!" Ember stomped forward and snatched a bag out of the jester's hands. "Those are mine."

Robby chuckled. "Then don't leave them lying around."

"Jerk. They were in my drawer." She shook a few pieces of whatever the contested food was into her hand and put the empty package on her dresser. Geraint took his spot in the rocking chair, so I perched on Ember's bed. She joined me, leaning her shoulder into mine.

That she was so comfortable with me lifted my mood, and I put my arm around her waist, pulling her against me. Ember fit perfectly tucked into my side, and the trusting way she leaned her head against my shoulder made me not want to move for fear of disturbing such a perfect moment.

Robby smiled slyly when he noticed her curl into my arms. I glanced at Geraint, but he looked unperturbed.

"So, where is he?" Ember asked.

"Our dear Dio has somehow gotten himself locked into an assisted living center for intellectually challenged adults," Robby said.

"He what now?" Ember stiffened in my arms.

"I'm not sure the details," Robby explained. "I believe tomorrow we should plan on visiting the center and verifying if it is in fact Dio. Then we must swing by the museum he was attempting to rob and see if we can find out why. If he doesn't simply tell us himself."

"Wait... what?" Ember sighed. "I'm so confused."

"Frankly, so am I," I admitted.

Robby nodded. "Yes. And, as I'm sure Ash will inform you, many of the records are incomplete or lost."

"So we leave first thing in the morning?" Geraint asked.

"I think that would be best. Perhaps you can endeavor to get both Ember and Prince Nic out of bed at a semi-decent hour."

Geraint laughed. "I feel they might tie me up with their shadows and shove me in a closet."

I caught a flash of pink as Ember licked her lips. There were a lot of other things I might want to do with our shadows other than tie up Geraint, and the knight was kind enough to give us plenty of time together, but I didn't correct him. I was not a morning person.

"I think we can make early happen once in a while," Ember said, her hand going to my thigh. "Is there anything else?"

"No."

"Great, go find Casey. She was looking for you. If you break her heart, I'll break you," Ember threatened.

"Mmmm, you're sexy when you're threatening," I said. It just slipped out, but I didn't regret the words when she slid her hand up my thigh.

"Yes, your highness. I shall also inform your parents that you're unavailable for a day or two." Robby bowed and left Ember's room, ignoring my comment.

I curled shadows around Ember's legs. She glanced up at me, eyes glinting mischievously.

Geraint noticed and got to his feet, the rocking chair creaking as he did so. Ember reached out with her shadows and twined one around Geraint's leg. He froze, glanced at me then at Ember.

"Spark," he whispered, his Irish lilt softening. "We had time earlier, and I know what's on your mind."

The shadow dissipated. "Okay, fine." Ember pushed her lip out in an adorable display of pique.

I glanced at Ember's drawings that Geraint and Ember had tacked to the walls of their room. Most of them featured the knight if it wasn't a drawing of a landscape.

"Perhaps you should enjoy the evening with your knight. I can certainly occupy myself elsewhere."

"I should keep watch." Geraint moved toward the door.

"One of you needs to stay," Ember pouted.

I hadn't moved despite offering to leave. I remembered a request she'd made when we'd first come together about joining her and Geraint for some kinky aerial sex. We hadn't had time to try any of that, but maybe we could try something similar now.

"I believe you requested some joint activities," I said quietly.

Geraint raised his eyebrows.

"Uh, I did, but, like, really, only if you're both comfortable with it."

"I'm not entirely sure either of us will ever truly be comfortable with it unless we try," I offered.

"Geraint?" She glanced at the knight.

He studied me for a long moment, expression guarded, before he shifted his attention to Ember and his entire being softened. "We can give it a try."

"Seriously, only if you're fine with it." Ember sucked her lower lip into her mouth.

I wanted nothing more than to pull that concerned expression from her face and replace it with one of ecstasy.

"We'll try," I said gently. "If we don't like it, then we don't have to do it again."

"Agreed," the knight said.

"Great!" Ember bounced on the edge of the bed.

I curled my shadows around her legs, reveling in the feel of her warmth against the cool wisps of essence. I didn't even have to touch her with my hands to feel her pulse racing faster, the faint squirm of anticipation as my tentacles worked their way higher.

The quiet moan that escaped her lips as her eyes fluttered shut had me instantly hard. I sent more shadows to support her as she lay back on the bed.

"How do you want to do this, Knight?" I couldn't help teasing Ember while I talked to Geraint.

"I'll follow your lead." He hung back, gaze darting between me and Ember uncertainly.

"You know what Ember likes better than I do."

"Mmm, I'm flexible, an aerialist, and you have shadow powers. Let's get creative," she murmured, gasping as one of my shadows slid inside her, curling, teasing her before sliding out again.

"Fuck, that feels so good," she groaned.

"So what you're saying is we should hang you upside down?" Geraint said with a mischievous light in his eyes.

"I could be convinced," Ember said. "For a few minutes, anyway."

Geraint shot a quick glance my way before he kneeled on the bed next to Ember. "Let's get your clothing off first."

I released her from my grip long enough for Geraint to efficiently strip her.

"Maybe lock the door? Just in case," Ember said as I wrapped her up in a web of shadows.

Geraint complied.

"Ready?" I trailed fingers down her chest, teasing one of her nipples. I'd fashioned my harness something like a shibari tie I'd seen in someone's dream, which left her breasts accented and deliciously on display, her light-colored skin a stark contrast with the black shadows that crisscrossed her body.

"Flip me," Ember replied with a grin.

I gently raised my princess with my powers and hung her upside down, spreading her legs to take advantage of her flexibility.

"Your highness, stand in front of her," Geraint suggested.

Curious about the order, but willing to comply, I did.

"Clothes, off," Ember ordered.

I melted my clothing away. Ember grabbed my hips and jerked me toward her.

"Lift me just a bit."

As soon as Ember floated a bit higher, she grasped my cock and brought it to her mouth.

"Oh," I gasped, in sudden understanding. My knees went weak as she wrapped those soft lips around me and sucked.

Geraint came up behind Ember and ran his hands across her thighs until he could fondle her gently, then more vigorously, sliding his finger inside of her.

She moaned around my cock. That sensation along with the view of Geraint finger-fucking her right in front of my face was incredible. Only long years of practice allowed me to keep Ember suspended while she treated me to the most intense pleasure I'd yet experienced, short of being inside her.

I was on the verge of spilling into her mouth, but I didn't want to end things that quickly.

"Ember, luv," I gasped.

She eased up, as if knowing what I wanted.

"That was incredible."

Geraint dipped another finger into my princess.

Hesitantly, I lowered my mouth to her clit and sucked and we both brought her trembling to the edge of release. When she spilled over, her body convulsed, and I was glad my dick was no longer in her mouth as she cried out.

Even upside down, her juices coated her with her release.

"Okay, upright, please."

I slowly twisted her upright, reveling in the way she hung limply in my web of shadows, trusting me completely to hold her off the ground.

Geraint went to his knees behind her, and I watched the expression of bliss part her lips and dilate her eyes as he worked his fingers over her soaked folds.

I tilted Ember slowly so Geraint would have better access and he shot me a grateful look before he buried his face in her pussy. I went to work worshiping her glorious breasts. They were a perfect handful, and I rolled her nipples between my fingers, watching her squirm in my grip.

She had enough room to squirm, but not enough to get away from our ministrations, and I thought we might be straying into territory that required a safe word. For now, any command she gave, I'd follow, and if we wanted to truly explore other possibilities later, we could set something up.

My nerves were alight with sensations as she writhed in my web of shadows. Every touch of her hot skin against the cool essence, every tremble, every gasp of her breath, sent pleasure coursing through me. It was as if my entire body were prepared to come undone. I needed to be inside her. Especially when she shattered again, crying Geraint's name.

"Nic, if you turn her toward you, you can take her from behind. She likes that a lot."

"How will you take her?" I made myself ask.

"She has a mouth." Geraint winked. He hadn't undressed yet, but when I nodded agreement, he shed his clothing. The Nightmare beings that had created the knight hadn't skimped. I was glad for Ember's sake.

Ember moaned encouragement. "Yes, that," she gasped.

I turned her in the air. She was completely limp in my grasp, letting me bend her limbs however I liked. I folded her as if she would be on her knees were she not hanging a few feet in the air, and lined her up with my cock at just the perfect height. Geraint went in front of her, and I freed her arms enough so she could grab his hips and position him how she liked.

The knight sucked in a breath as Ember wrapped those sweet lips around his girth and took him all the way. She'd clearly had a lot of practice, which I'd already benefited from. I imagined the way those lips had felt on me, then slid inside her wet pussy. She was soaked, but I gave her a moment to adjust to my size before pulling out and thrusting into her again.

She squealed and wiggled against me.

I paused, concerned.

"That was a good squeal, keep going," Geraint said, voice rough with lust.

I pounded into her, pulling a few extra tentacles of shadow and wrapping them around her, squeezing, caressing, bringing one forward to play with her clit, and tickling her other hole with another. I wasn't sure how she felt about that, so I didn't enter.

Though I was closer to the knight than I'd ever expected to get, it felt natural to share Ember like this. He had his eyes shut, mouth parted and somehow his presence added to our experience. Sharing like this, with another man Ember truly loved, was better than I could have imagined.

Ember's trembles grew more urgent and though her mouth was full of the knight, she was crying my name around his dick.

Ember's muscles clamped down on my cock, trapping me, triggering a powerful orgasm I couldn't have held back if I'd tried, as she rocketed into her own release.

My cry was wordless. Geraint swore as she brought him along for the ride.

"Oh, my gods," Ember said after she released the knight. "That was amazing."

"I don't have words." My limbs trembled.

Geraint stood there with his head down, powerful legs braced to keep him upright. I saw that I'd extended my web of tentacles to wrap around him as well, and quickly withdrew them.

I slid out of my princess, groaning as she quivered in my grip. Once we were free, I slowly lowered her to the ground until she supported herself on her hands and knees, then I allowed myself to flow down onto the floor next to her, gathering Ember into my arms so we could cuddle while we recovered.

She held out her hand to Geraint, and I nodded when he looked at me. He lay down on the other side and we spooned our princess between us.

"Maybe next time put me down in the bed." Ember laughed.

"It is a good thing you have a comfortable floor," I replied with a chuckle. "I wasn't going to make it to your bed." Her skin shivered as I ran my fingers over the faint marks I'd left from the weave of essence I'd held her in.

"Fair enough, my prince. Geraint?"

"The possibilities are quite endless," he replied. "As long as Nic can stay focused enough to keep you in the air."

"I will tell you if we ever truly test my limits," I assured them.

"So we get to do this again?" Ember sounded so hopeful.

I smoothed some of her hair off her sweat slicked shoulder. "Yes, luv, if you and Geraint want to."

"All the time." She stretched between us, her skin sliding along mine enticingly.

"Anything for you, Ember," Geraint replied.

"Same," she answered sleepily, kissing him on the shoulder.

"We should get cleaned up before we fall asleep on the floor." I forced my eyes open.

"Oh, yes! After-sex shower sex is the best sex!" My princess perked right up at that idea.

I raised my eyebrows and glanced at Geraint. He chuckled and shrugged. "She's not wrong, and we do have a big shower."

"I'd be honored to join you," I said.

Ember climbed somewhat unsteadily to her feet and headed for the bathroom. "Don't keep me waiting!"

Geraint and I both laughed and followed.

Dakota Brown

CHAPTER 4

Ember

Since returning from Nightmare, I hadn't been off the property except to explore the woods. Leaving the sanctuary of my childhood home and the summer camp, not to mention the miles of wilderness, felt surreal. I stared out the window of our van while Robby drove. Geraint and Nic sat in the back.

The woods gave way to farmland, then we hit the first small town. For a while, I felt like we were on our horseback journey through the boundary lands between Nightmare and Dream. The silver-hooved, white horses that had carried us had been remarkable. Then I remembered Nic mentioning that the nothingness storms had gotten worse. Were the horses all right? The wolves that had carried us? I even had a passing worry about the frightening clouds that had chased us.

Not to mention the land itself. If we could stop the destruction, would we be able to repair what was erased, or was it gone for good?

The first town we reached was a small farm town that many of the locals went to for groceries and a handful of restaurants. It also catered to the antiquing and flea market crowd and a fair bit of traffic from the larger city nearby wandered the streets looking for relatively ancient treasures. At least by local standards.

I window shopped as we crawled through downtown. Old rusty wagon wheels, wooden carts that had seen better days but looked great as decoration, sewing machines, creepy dolls, a mirror I tried to peer into even though we were at the wrong angle and in a car on the road, all sorts of interesting things to check out.

My gaze strayed back to one window when movement caught my attention. *Hadn't that doll been facing the other way?*

I shivered.

We had to stop at the one traffic light in town while a pair of older men hobbled across the street. One of them stopped in front of our van and stared.

"Did his eyes just flash?" I sank down in my seat.

Robby's knuckles went white on the steering wheel. "Not sure," he muttered.

We both relaxed marginally when the street cleared, and we could continue. As soon as we cleared the one busy section of main street, we picked up the pace again and were soon out of town.

"Should we be paranoid?" I twisted my hands together, hating the curl of fear that trickled from my sternum to my stomach and sent cold chills to my extremities.

"Yes," Robby replied, his voice devoid of his usual jovial sarcasm.

"Shit," I replied.

Nic, sitting behind me, reached forward and squeezed my shoulder. "Nightmare may be turning against us, but we're not without our own power and resources."

"Words I never needed to hear," Robby muttered. "Nightmare turning against us. The place is creepy and dangerous enough without it being intentionally hostile."

"You're just filling me with warm fuzzies," I replied.

"We're on the interstate now," Robby said. "It'll be all right." He flipped on the radio to an upbeat pop rock station and softly hummed along with the music.

I looked out the window for a while, tension rolling through my muscles and knotting my back. Exhausted, I finally shut my eyes and used my knuckles to rub them.

"Ember, we'll be okay," Geraint said.

I crossed my arms and sank down into my seat, not sure if I was sulking or hiding. After another thirty minutes, Robby slowed and took an exit. We were nearing the city and traffic had picked up, but we were still very much in the country when we exited. Cleared farmland broken by the occasional thick stand of trees dominated our view. I had to force myself to keep from staring into the depths of the shadows, looking for lurking nightmares.

The trees gave way to vast cornfields. I stared at them. Something was strange about the fields, but I couldn't place what it was.

Robby slowed as we approached a side road. He turned the van and hesitated before driving between the towering corn on either side of the road.

"That's it! Why the hell is the corn so tall? It's supposed to be 'knee high by the fourth of July.'" I shivered as the radio crackled, losing reception.

Robby hit the brakes before taking a breath and accelerating again. "Better just to get through it. Perhaps a pocket of Nightmare? Maybe something else."

Nothing happened as we passed through the abnormally tall corn, though I swear the sky darkened. Some of the stalks swayed as if in the wind. Maybe it was from the car's movement?

We all sighed in relief when we came out of the corn on the other side of the fields. Acres of rolling grassy fields lay between us and our destination, a large, squarish brick building. It didn't look particularly inviting, but it also wasn't a dump. The grounds went from mowed grass to lightly tended flower beds with benches and tables interspersed. A wide concrete path wound through the gardens and led back to the building. Trees provided shade, but the broad expanse of grass would make it hard to sneak up to the care facility. Hopefully, sneaking wouldn't be necessary.

Robby pulled into a parking area, and we got out. Even Nic. He winced at the bright sun, but didn't complain. Robby led the way, Nic took my hand, and Geraint trailed behind, watching our backs.

No one was outside, but I could imagine it might be lunch time for the residents. The light breeze and the relatively low humidity made it pleasant enough in the shade, so there had to be a reason everyone was inside.

Still creeped out, I followed Robby into the entryway. He held the door for all of us, then took the lead up to the receptionist's desk. It was cool inside, heavily air-conditioned. The woman behind the desk appeared normal enough, large glasses perched on a pert nose. She had a friendly smile on her face, and a sweater to ward off the chill from the AC.

The rest of the entry into the facility was a bit more intimidating. The door behind her opened with a keypad and all the glass looked heavy, like it might be bullet proof. The décor was spare, but appeared comfortable. All in all, very contradictory.

"How can I help you?" the woman asked once we stood in front of the desk.

"My name is Robby McClain. I called ahead. We have an appointment to meet with Dio."

"Ahh, you're the folks who think you might know him." She sounded a tad suspicious.

"Yes, dear Dio. We went to high school together and only recently learned of his disability and presence here.

We weren't especially close, but we were friends and thought we should stop in and check on him."

The last bit smoothed the worry lines from the woman's forehead. Close friends would probably have been suspicious after all this time.

"I should warn you, he's not coherent most of the time. The doctors can't find anything wrong with him."

"Thank you, Ms."—Robby peered at her nametag—"Peterson. Very helpful." He turned up the charm, and she smiled in return.

"Samantha is coming up to get you. Due to the nature of his residency here, it has to be a supervised visit."

"Not a problem," Robby assured her.

Moments later, the secure door clicked open, and a young woman came out that I could only describe as wholesome. She had brown her hair cut in a bob and wore a soft, neutral-toned sweater and skirt with leggings underneath. Even her smile was relaxing.

Except I was still on edge from the strange cornfield, and I fought against the peace she exuded, determined to stay alert for danger.

I glanced at Nic, and he squeezed my fingers, but the skin at the corners of his eyes creased and his gaze shifted from spot to spot, never resting. He felt as uneasy as I did. Geraint put his hand on my shoulder for a moment before moving between me and the entry door.

"Hello, Robby," Samantha said, her voice cheerful. "And you're Ember? And Nic and Geraint?" She mangled Geraint's name, and he quietly corrected her. His Irish lilt and his captivating smile made her eyes light up.

"He does have a dangerously sexy smile," Nic leaned over and whispered in my ear.

I glanced up at my prince and arched an eyebrow. He winked at me.

"It's nice to meet you all. If you'll follow me?"

We went through the security door. I flinched when it clicked shut behind me, feeling closed in, trapped. I pressed my free hand to my stomach.

"We can still get out," Nic assured me in another quiet whisper.

I took a deep breath and tried to calm my racing heart. Being trapped had never been something that had worried me before. Freaking not-Baz.

The décor was simple. Nothing loose, but someone had painted pictures on the walls in the place of framed art. Quiet music filtered through the air, something soothing. It would have driven me nuts after a while, and I wondered if it was truly effective. I felt like I was in some sort of hotel. The doors were all heavy, locked, and numbered. Each one had a plastic wall file with colorful folders in them.

At the end of the hallway, we crowded into an elevator, and Samantha scanned a keycard, entered a code, and pushed four. Dio was on the top floor? The level of security seemed excessive for a place that wasn't a hospital, but maybe I had misunderstood the type of facility this was.

Nic and Robby had nearly identical frowns on their faces, as if they concentrated hard and didn't like what they sensed.

The elevator slowed, and a chime dinged as we reached the fourth floor. I wasn't sure what I expected when the doors slid open, but I held my breath. The décor was the same and, though the hallways were straight, I felt like I could get lost in here. Especially since I couldn't figure out the system behind the numbers on the doors. They seemed completely random. I wasn't even convinced I was actually on the fourth floor because some of the numbers started with three or two and nothing was sequential.

Samantha led us about halfway down the corridor and scanned her keycard before knocking on the door and pushing it open.

"Dio," she called as she entered the room.

The hotel impression didn't diminish as we went inside. Narrow hallway entrance with a bathroom next to it, generic coloration, and décor. Again, nothing that could be easily thrown around other than a few chairs, which, on second glance, might have been bolted to the floor.

A darker-skinned man with short, very curly hair and a scruffy beard sat hunched in a comfortable-looking armchair and stared at the wall. He wore a blue polo shirt and faded blue jeans. He didn't react to Samantha's call, but when I came into the room, he tilted his head and his gaze fixed on me.

"Princess," he said.

Samantha glanced at me, eyes widening slightly before she put a hand on Dio's arm. "Dio, this is Ember. Princess is not an appropriate form of address."

What little animation his eyes had held dulled, and he nodded. "Ember." Even his voice sounded flatter.

What the fuck?

"And this is Nic, Robby, and Geraint. They're old friends of yours here to visit. Isn't that nice of them?"

"Very nice," Dio agreed, with the mild Middle Eastern accent I remembered from our childhood.

Nic squeezed my hand before letting go. He walked to Dio's side and went down on one knee, taking his brother's hand.

"Dio, how are you feeling?"

The question seemed to confuse Dio for a moment, furrows creasing his brow. He looked at Samantha before looking back at his brother. "Fine."

He spoke as if forcing the words out.

Geraint took Nic's place next to me, holding me back when I tried to go to Dio.

"Just a minute, Spark," Geraint said.

Robby went over to Samantha and put an arm over her shoulder. "We're going to need some privacy," he said.

She opened her mouth to object, but he placed his hand in front of her eyes. The woman froze. Like, I wasn't even sure she was breathing.

I stared at the jester, mouth open in shock.

"Robby?" I finally squeaked out.

"What, princess?" he replied. "We need privacy, and something fishy is obviously going on here."

"I just..." I shook my head. "How did you do that?"

He shrugged with a sly grin. "Trade secret."

I glanced at Nic, but he stared at his brother, eyes narrowed.

"Diokophobia," he said sharply.

Dio's eyes sharpened briefly. "Nic, danger. Baz is not Baz, and our Princess must come home." He leaned forward, grabbing Nic's shoulder, his hand sinking in as Nic briefly faded to shadow.

"Our Princess is safe. We're working on saving Baz. We need to get you out of here, Dio."

Dio sank back into his armchair, eyes going glassy and vacant.

"Have they drugged him?" I asked. Geraint finally let go of my shoulder, and I went to Dio's side.

Nic took my hand and placed it on Dio's arm.

"He feels... empty." Unable to help myself, I jerked my hand away from Dio's cool arm.

"His essence is gone."

"What?" That sounded bad.

"His Nightmare essence is gone," Nic repeated himself. "I wasn't even sure it was possible to survive without it."

"Yes, gone," Dio murmured. "Had to protect the essence. If they get it all, everything is lost."

"What did you do with it, Dio?" Nic tightened his grip on his brother.

"Hid it away. Safe amongst pretty sparkly gems of light." He smiled, as if remembering something pleasant.

"Gems of light?" Geraint said. "What does that mean?"

No one had an answer, and it seemed Dio was done talking. I even tried touching his skin again, but he remained locked in that distant smile.

"Shit, that's weird," I said.

"Yes," Robby agreed. "Very."

"So, what do we do?" I glanced around his room, then frowned as a half-seen shine caught my eye. "Could this be on camera?"

"Oh, shit," Robby muttered. "Damn humans."

"Nothing to be done about it now," Nic replied. "We should reserve any further discussion for later."

Robby nodded, passed his hand in front of Samantha's face, and she came alert with a confused squint before her previously cheerful expression returned.

"He's not very responsive, I'm afraid," she said.

"Yeah, well, we wanted to make sure he was being cared for. We can't fault his surroundings," Robby replied.

I felt sick and couldn't bring myself to try and come up with anything positive to say. Fortunately, Robby had everything under control.

"We're just leaving him here?" I whispered when Samantha led us to the door.

"For now," Nic replied just as quietly.

The hair on the back of my neck rose, and my shoulders knotted. It felt like at any moment someone was going to detain us, but we made it to the main security door with no issues. Samantha let us out. We said a brief goodbye to the receptionist and then headed out into the hot afternoon humidity.

Robby hit the remote start on the van, so it wasn't a million degrees inside when we climbed in.

When I opened my mouth to pepper the guys with questions, Robby held up his hand.

Annoyed, but trusting that they knew what they were doing, I stayed silent.

The too-tall cornfields felt especially ominous when we drove through them, but we pulled out onto the main road without incident.

"That was fucking weird," I said.

"Yeah," Geraint agreed.

"So what's going on?" I glanced at Robby.

"Not sure, Princess."

"It appears to be a pocket of space where the conscious and unconscious realm overlap. The two people we encountered were human, near as I could tell, but there was a great deal of energy of the Dream realm in that place. Not Dream essence, per say. Just the feel of Dream," Nic explained. "I wasn't aware such places existed."

"Wow," I murmured. "So, what's up with the creepy-ass cornfield?"

"Protection, most likely," Robby said. "Or a deterrent. Even the twins, and the tooth fairies avoid going into the Nightmare cornfields. It might be similar here."

"I don't even know what to ask."

"Don't go into the corn," Nic insisted.

An involuntary shudder wracked my body. "Okay, right." Somehow, I didn't think they were joking, either.

"So, what do we do?"

"About Dio? Nothing, right now," Robby said.

"But—"

"There's not much we can do until we find out what he did with his essence," Nic said. "He needs to be whole before we can rescue him. If we took him out of there now, we'd have to care for him and they're not obviously mistreating my brother. I'm also not entirely sure how to get him out while he's in his current state. Once he's whole, we can break him out."

"Did anyone notice the complete lack of mirrors in that place?" Geraint pointed out.

"I had," Robby replied.

I hadn't, but now that Geraint mentioned it, I hadn't seen one in the bathroom attached to Dio's bedroom.

"So, how do we figure out where he put his essence?" I sighed as traffic slowed now that we were much closer to the city.

"I'm guessing we'll find clues at the museum," Robby answered.

"Makes sense." I glanced at my phone. We weren't far, as long as the traffic didn't jam up.

***

"Bless the inventor of air conditioning," I muttered as we wandered around the cool museum.

It wasn't crowded, and we went from exhibit to exhibit, trying to figure out what Dio had been interested in when he'd been arrested. The records Ash had tracked down hadn't said.

"As they could capture Dio, he had likely already separated his essence from his person," Robby said.

"Are we sure he did it voluntarily?" Geraint was on hand-holding duty while Nic slipped from shadow to shadow, able to cover more ground that way, and I was grateful for the reassuring grip.

"Reasonably," Robby said. "Based on his response."

"Was he talking about stars?" I'd been thinking about Dio's words. It killed me to see my childhood friend in such a strange and debilitated condition, but when we passed the exhibit entrance for the planetarium, his comment about light came to mind.

"Possibly," Robby agreed. We turned into the exhibit. There weren't any shows for an hour, but I didn't really think that was our destination, anyway.

We explored the other space exhibits for a while, but nothing obvious jumped out at us.

"Ember."

I yelped as Nic stepped out of a shadow.

Geraint twitched, as if about to defend me, but Robby didn't react. Perhaps he'd sensed Nic coming?

"Yes?" I asked once I caught my breath.

"Come with me," Nic said.

I followed my prince. Robby and Geraint trailed along behind us.

He led us out of the astronomy exhibit and up a flight of stairs to the gems and minerals. I went in, breath already taken away at the beauty of the various minerals on display.

"Gems of light," I whispered.

"Yes," Nic agreed. "See if you find anything here."

Nodding, I let my eyes rove over the displays, moving from case to case as slowly as I could make myself, though excitement hurried my steps.

I reached out with my new abilities, touching the shadows that hid amongst the bright lights. Something to my right called to me, and I followed the tug on my senses.

Before long, I came to a case in the back of the exhibit area. It was a heavily protected case full of priceless gems on loan from private collections. A guard stood nearby. My eyes were immediately drawn to a dark blue stone that sparkled with thousands of lights about the size of my fist. It was round and oh, so beautiful. I didn't point, but I glanced at Nic. He nodded.

"What do we do?" I looked around, but no one seemed overly interested in us.

Nic put his index finger to his lips as he thought. "I'm not sure."

Robby joined us, studying the gems in the case. "Well, that sure is pretty."

I noticed he didn't let his gaze linger on any of the pretty minerals for long. I pulled my attention away from what had to be the physical manifestation of Dio's essence. He was right. We didn't know if we were alone or not.

A reflection in the glass caught my attention. I froze, meeping softly as I tried to contain a scream. The big red nose matched the angry red eyes and contrasted sharply with pale skin. Big, poofy, plastic-looking hair in multiple colors framed the wide, angry smile. *Fucking hell.* I put my hand over my mouth and twisted around, expecting to find a horror movie clown looming over my shoulder. Nothing.

Well, there were people. One of them, a taller man wearing a gray suit, stared at us. His intense gaze felt as if it burned a hole through me, and his amused smirk sent shivers down my spine.

When I looked back at the glass, just before Geraint grabbed my arm and dragged me away, I again saw that creepy-ass clown, with the same amused smirk on its face. *What the hell?*

"We are being followed," Robby pointed out unnecessarily.

"No shit," I growled. "Did you see the creepy-ass clown?"

Robby's eyes widened. "I did not."

"Then who the hell else is following us?"

"Vampires," the jester replied tightly. "Furious ones."

I whimpered. "Which is worse, the vampires or the clown?"

"The clown," Nic replied.

"Why are they after us now?"

"Well, either they think we can lead them to the things they're after, or we already have, and they simply want us dead," Robby answered, sounding almost jovial as we pushed our way through the crowd.

"Seriously?" I muttered.

"I'm always serious, Spark. You know that," Robby said.

We headed for the stairs, but at the last minute Geraint jerked me away, and Nic and Robby followed. I still couldn't see what was after us, but I trusted the men. I just hoped we weren't going to get captured. I'd cause a disturbance that would make the news to avoid that ever happening again.

Nic led us to another part of the museum. We hurried into the display and pulled up short as the dude in the suit with the creepy smile blocked our way.

Every reflective surface showed the same clown I'd seen before, pointed teeth bared.

"Oh, my god," I breathed.

We spun around, but two women and a man blocked the exit. They looked normal enough, wearing jeans, t-shirts, and tennis shoes, but all three of them were unnaturally attractive, and they moved with a fluid grace most dancers couldn't match. Even they cast uneasy glances at the man behind us.

"Though I normally quite like games," the man said, voice cruelly amused. "Today, I simply want answers. Where is he, and what are you doing here?"

They didn't know. Or at least these beings didn't. But then what kind of facility was the mental institute?

"Why are you working for the enemy?" I said, instead of answering. "They're trying to destroy your world."

The clown snorted. "We don't need Nightmare as it is to survive. The fears and dreams of humans feed us more than enough to keep us alive."

"Without Dream, humans won't survive," I argued.

"Dream will never vanish." The clown shrugged. "And sometimes change is good."

"They're erasing the land," I protested.

His smile deepened. "To remake it."

Okay, fine, he didn't care.

"Where is he? Last chance." The reflected clowns began juggling something metallic and shiny. Drops of red fell from the reflections' fingers.

"Who?" Robby asked with a yawn, as if he didn't have a care in the world.

Instead of answering, the clown gestured. All of the insects pinned to boards or otherwise displayed in the collection clattered their wings behind the glass.

Even the fossilized ones.

My throat closed, and my lungs apparently stopped working. I grabbed at my chest, trying to get a breath out. "What the fuck?" I gasped again when I finally managed to suck in some air.

It didn't help that I saw the vampires edge backward, eyes darting from case to case uneasily.

Nic swirled into mist, and I wished I could join him. He hadn't left me. He'd simply gone to a more defensible state. Geraint flexed his hands and cast about as if looking for a weapon.

I tried not to whimper, feeling useless. My tenuous control over the shadow essence failed me completely. I huddled against Geraint's back and hoped my knight could protect me. The damsel in distress feeling wasn't a comfortable one, but I wasn't a fighter. I was a dancer and currently completely out of my element.

51

"You will give me Diokophobia," the clown hissed. He threw his hands out in a grandiose gesture that the reflection clowns mimicked. The objects they juggled flew outward, along with a spray of blood. The glass cases shattered.

I winced at the tremendous crack and covered my face, knowing it was a futile attempt to save myself from the shrapnel.

Nic swirled his essence around us, deflecting most of the glass.

He solidified next to me, wavering. The prince put a hand to his face and wiped away a smear of blood. Then another. He fell to one knee, and I went to the ground with him, grabbing his arm. My hand came away from his semi-solid arm, wet with blood. He'd taken the brunt of the glass for us. It hadn't killed him, because he was at least partially made of shadow, but it obviously hadn't been good for him either.

"Nic!"

The clown laughed. The insects with wings a-clatter took to the air and dove at us.

I shrieked and shoved my essence at Nic, hoping it would help him recover so we could get out of here.

"I'm all right, Ember," he gasped.

"Great, because we need to get out of here." Robby had pulled a sword from nowhere and swung the white blade through the air, batting at insects. He couldn't possibly get them all, and my skin crawled as I brushed them away, frantically.

Geraint grabbed me under the arms and pulled me to my feet.

Nic struggled back to his, and we sprinted for the exit, only to come up against the wide-eyed vampires.

They bared fangs, and one licked his lips at the smell of blood in the air.

Insects dove at us from behind.

Robby and Geraint went for the vampires.

The clown's chilling fingernails-on-slate laughter grated against my ears, sending prickles down my spine and piercing my eardrums until all I could hear was that and the clack of wings. I screamed as an insect with a particularly large stinger dove at my face.

Geraint batted it away and pulled me behind him.

One of the vampires grabbed for me. Nic punched the creature in the face and the vampire jerked back, staggering and clutching his nose.

The insects formed up into a cloud and dove directly for Nic. He melted completely into shadow as they attacked him. Through our bond, I could feel his agony. Apparently, like the glass, dissipating hadn't helped him as much as it should have.

One vampire screamed before bursting into dust. Robby used the momentum from his decapitating swing to spin around and take out a few of the bugs.

Before the dust cloud of dead vampire disappeared completely, the clown held out his hands and called it to him.

I had thought I couldn't get any more terrified. I was wrong.

The dust coalesced back into the vampire it had once been, except the skin sagged off bones, revealing gaping holes, some that went all the way to the other side, and insects flew through the gaps. It staggered forward, snapping rotted teeth at us.

The remaining two vampires stared at each other for a moment.

"Nope!" the women both shouted, and they vanished.

"Fuck!" I screamed.

The zombie vampire charged forward, faster even than the insects.

"Run, princess!" Robby shouted, facing the thing with his sword, Geraint at his side.

Nic grabbed my arm and pulled me away.

I ran.

CHAPTER 5

Ember

I didn't know where to go. Other exhibits had come to life. Museum patrons scattered, leaving only animated things coming after us. Swords from the weaponry displays flew through the air, creatures lumbered or ran, snakes slithered in our direction.

A fucking zombie king cobra nearly stopped my heart when it reared up in front of me.

Nic grabbed me around the waist, and we leaped off the balcony into space. I didn't even question him as we hurtled toward the ground. This was far preferable to the creatures.

He threw his hand out, and tendrils of shadow connected us to some scaffolding. He grunted as we hit the end of our arc, but we slowed enough that we didn't crash into the ground. Nic held all my weight and set me down gently before rubbing his shoulder.

"You okay?" I touched Nic's hand.

"Not really." He glanced around. "I'm a prince of Nightmare. I'm a literal nightmare. You would think things like this wouldn't bother me."

"I feel like this is a little extreme," I replied.

"A little," he agreed with a strained chuckle.

We had a moment of reprieve before this level of the museum came alive around us. "This is insane!" I shouted.

I took off running, but the ground warped under my feet, and I went sprawling. The glass surfaces of the remaining displays turned to mirrors and threw my perception into chaos. I had no idea which way to go.

"Even more insane! Nic, what do we do?"

My prince pulled me to my feet, and I collapsed against his chest as the ground heaved. When I looked again, the flooring had turned into some sort of black-and-white lined illusion, and my head spun just looking at it. Dizzy, I shut my eyes.

"I really hate clowns," Nic muttered.

"This way," a quiet voice broke through the noise.

I risked opening my eyes.

A translucent woman stood there, wearing spectacles in place on a prominent nose, a long dress with an apron over it, and a kind smile. She held a book in her hand.

"Librarian?" I guessed.

"Yes. The books are safe. Come this way."

Not having a better idea, Nic and I followed the ghost. We kept our eyes on her, which helped us stagger through the museum.

Finally, the ground returned to the normal polished granite, and the exhibits normalized. We picked up speed until she led us into some back rooms amongst stacks of ancient books and documents.

"You are safe here. The creatures cannot enter. Wait. I will get your friends."

Tears leaking from my eyes, I collapsed to the ground and gasped for breath. Nic sank to his knees next to me and pulled me against his chest while I sobbed.

"Clowns are difficult to fight," Nic offered. "Even in Nightmare. This one probably lives in the conscious realm. The vampires, too. It's possible they've never even been to Nightmare. Especially powerful dreams can form right here in the conscious realm. Normally, we would recruit the more powerful Nightmares and Dreams loyal to the Dream realm to help keep creatures like this in check, or even return them to where they belong. Sometimes they get out of hand. I suspect most of the Nightmares here welcome the change. They'll be freer to act however they want."

"Well, if they are nightmares and dreams, it kind of makes sense that they'd want the freedom to run amok," I forced out between sobs.

"Yes."

"Why are we talking about this now?"

"Because only one of us can break down into tears, and you beat me to it."

His admission startled a laugh from me. I nearly choked on my own spit, but I felt a lot better suddenly.

Nic hugged me and kissed my temple. "She found the others. They're a little beat up, but they're coming."

"Thank you for protecting me," I said, voice small.

"Of course, Ember. You're my princess. I'll do anything in my power to keep you safe."

Robby and Geraint joined us after a few more minutes. Robby managed to look artfully disheveled, his wavy brown hair disarrayed, a thin cut across his cheek seeping blood, his shirt torn in just the right spot to look heroic, like some sort of romance novel hero. I snorted.

Geraint looked a little worse for the wear, a bruise discoloring his cheek, his shirt torn badly, splotchy patches of blood staining the ruined garment.

"Are you two okay?" I asked as soon as they came in.

They both nodded.

"Please tell me zombie vampire is really dust now."

"The librarian finished off the zombie vampire," Geraint replied, voice shellshocked.

"Oh, good." I shivered.

"She also drove off the clown," Robby supplied. "A very badass librarian."

"Good." I shifted off Nic, and we both got to our feet, just as the librarian appeared in the room with us.

"Quite the mess. You should be safe now, however."

"Our deepest gratitude," Nic said with a deep and regal bow. "How can we possibly repay you?"

The ghostly woman shook her head. "No need. All part of the job. We have a lot of work to do to repair the fabric of the museum. Perhaps you could leave, as you disrupt it, too. Come back tomorrow to finish your tour."

"Thank you," Nic said.

We left the records room the librarian had led us to. I noticed it looked a lot more like a modern storeroom than it had when we'd entered. Incongruously, the museum looked normal when we exited, with patrons slowly wandering from exhibit to exhibit. A few children darted around. It all seemed so ordinary.

"He warped reality around us, but actual reality remained untouched," Nic said.

"That... makes absolutely no sense." My brain refused to cope with this new information.

"No?" Nic squeezed my shoulder with his hand. "It will, eventually."

"Is that a threat or a promise?" I folded my arms across my chest and hugged myself.

"Maybe both," he admitted.

Geraint brushed my arm with his. Walking between the two men and following Robby, we left the building as the librarian had requested so she could fix the museum's fabric. Whatever that meant.

***

After a quick meal, we headed home. We had a lot of planning to do.

I'd drifted off into a troubled sleep, but jerked awake when the car skidded to a halt.

"What?" I murmured sleepily.

"The car stalled." Robby shoved the gearshift into park and turned off the key, though the van was already quiet. We opened the doors. It was much too hot to sit inside the vehicle with the doors closed while Robby popped the hood.

Geraint walked around us, alert for danger. We'd made it off the interstate and onto one of the back roads that would take us home. I knew where we were at, still about a half an hour from home.

Nic stayed in the van, lurking in the shadows. I sat on the back seat in the shade with the side door slid open and the prince shifted over until he could gently massage my neck.

"Mmmm, feels good," I murmured.

Robby messed around under the hood for a while before slamming it and trying to start the car again. Nothing. Not even a click.

"What's wrong?" I mumbled, lulled back to sleepiness by the heat and Nic's hands on my shoulders.

Geraint came over to my side of the van and put his hand on my leg. I threaded my fingers with his, and he squeezed gently. He'd found a spare shirt and didn't look quite so much like he'd been in a bar fight now.

"This is trouble," Robby replied. "I've called for a tow, but chances are we're dealing with another attack. There shouldn't be anything wrong with the van. It was just serviced."

We were miles from home, and at least a mile from the nearest farmhouse. A stand of trees marked the beginnings of the more heavily forested region, and the land rolled gently as we approached the mountain range. The temperature had climbed into the nineties, and the humidity beaded sweat on my brow. Insects screamed their summer songs and not much moved in the heat. The cornfield we'd parked by was normal length waist-high corn, and though all three of the Dream beings had eyed it warily, it apparently didn't bother them as much as the unnatural corn had.

"Ugh. Could they have at least left the air conditioning?" I grumbled.

"Or done this at night," Nic added softly.

"Yeah, that too." I put my free hand over his.

With both of my men touching me, I felt grounded and safe. I knew that was an illusion, but it helped a little.

That illusion shattered when Robby sprinted over to our side of the van, grabbed my arm, and tugged. "Let's go now!"

I let the jester yank me out of the van and urge me into a sprint down the road. Geraint and Nic followed. I didn't have the breath to ask what was going on, so I just followed, trusting my friend.

Moments later, a massive snap and crackle had us spinning around. The electric pole behind us broke in half and landed on the car.

The booming explosion that followed probably wasn't what would have happened in normal circumstances, but in this case, the van went up like it was in an action movie. The pressure wave shoved us forward, though we kept to our feet.

"Fuck," Robby snarled. "I liked that van."

"Please tell me we hadn't loaded any of the gear yet," I gasped, completely and somewhat unreasonably stressed about that. It could be replaced, but still...

"We hadn't," Robby assured me.

"Oh, good." That was something, anyway.

Lightning raced up the power line and struck the ground behind us.

"What the hell is that?" I shouted as I ran.

Snakes of blue lightning arced out from the downed power line.

Well, that was certainly some sort of nightmare. I ran harder.

Geraint swore. I saved my breath, though my energy flagged. I was in good shape, but extended sprints were not an activity I engaged in, well, ever.

Nic grabbed my arm and pushed some of his essence into me. With that energy boost, I kept up my speed until Robby slowed. We all stopped and looked behind us.

Tendrils of blue crawled along the ground as if searching for us.

"What do we do?" I panted, leaning over, and resting my hands on my thighs while I caught my breath.

"Call the authorities," Robby said. "Then call for a ride. It's the only thing we can do."

I pulled out my phone and debated who to call. My choices were my parents or Ash or Casey. Maybe Ash would be available.

I dialed her number, but the phone went to voicemail. She was probably in court. Hopefully, my parents weren't teaching right now.

Dad picked up on the second ring. "Hi, Spark."

"Hey, Dad, the van broke down just off the interstate. Any chance someone can come out and get us?"

"We'll send someone right now. Everyone okay?"

"Yeah. Just a breakdown." I didn't want to worry him over the phone.

"All right, honey. Be careful and we'll get someone out there to pick you four up."

"Thanks Dad. Love you."

"Love you, too, Spark."

If only he knew the day we'd had. I'd tell him some of it later.

"They coming?" Geraint put his arm around me.

"Yeah."

"Great. Robby is finished dealing with the police on the phone, and the blue power snakes have vanished."

Sighing, I leaned back into my partner's solid embrace. "Good." Our cuddle was short with the sun pounding down on us. I glanced over at Nic. The sun had leached most of the color from his complexion, and exhaustion tugged at his expression.

"Your highness, you should get out of the sun," Robby said, gesturing toward the tree line. It was much closer after our sprint away from the downed power lines.

Nic nodded, and after a quick glance at me, dissolved into wisps of shadow.

"The two of you should join him," Robby suggested. "Stay close to the road."

Wordlessly, Geraint and I trudged toward the tree line. We both eyed the power lines warily, but they stayed quiet. Plenty of people would be without power from this. Hopefully the power company would get out here quickly and fix everything.

We made it to the shelter of the trees without incident and joined Nic in the shade.

"Are you okay?" I went over to my prince and touched his arm. My hand sank into his shadowy form as if pressing into a cool gel.

"I am, thank you. I simply need rest after all the sunlight, and holding myself to one form for so long today. It is getting easier as I practice, but today took quite a bit of effort."

Geraint took up a position where he could watch the road and the woods at the same time. It put his back to the cornfield, but I could watch that for him. He noticed my attention and gave me a quick smile.

The cops, the fire department, and the power company showed up at about the same time. I snorted when I saw the police officer get out of her cruiser and scratch her head in confusion at the power pole lying across the top of the burned up van. Car fires were hot and fast, and it still smoldered, but the power pole had burned, and flames crept toward the corn.

The firefighters got busy, and Robby talked with the officer. Nic stayed with us until the officer got in her car and headed our direction. Geraint and I met her at the side of the road and answered a barrage of questions. For her part, she didn't seem suspicious, simply confused as to how a power pole could break in half like it had.

We didn't have any ideas that would make sense to a mundane human, and I'd been asleep until right before it had happened, so she left us with her business card.

Robby joined us just as one of the school vans came into view.

Casey stared at our ruined vehicle, eyes wide, while she slowed to pick us up.

"You said it broke down, not immolated," she exclaimed.

"Yeah. We didn't want to worry anyone and we're all fine, so we figured we'd tell the entire story when we got back." I shrugged. "I didn't think they'd send you out to pick us up."

"Oh, I volunteered. My classes were done for the day, anyway." Her gaze lingered on Robby.

Hiding smiles, Geraint and I climbed into the back. Nic joined us a moment later, looking vastly improved from before. Robby slid into the front passenger seat, thanking Casey profusely for her assistance.

Someone was getting laid tonight if he wanted it, by the doe-eyed look Casey was giving the jester. Geraint had an entertained half-smile on his face, and I sensed Nic's amusement through our bond. I hoped Robby was careful with her.

Lulled by the cool air conditioning and Robby's quiet conversation with Casey, I drifted back to sleep until we reached the school and home.

Mom met us in the parking area. "What happened?" she asked when we got out.

I let my gaze slide toward Casey, hoping she'd catch the significance before I answered. "It was the weirdest thing." Maybe that would clue her in if my look hadn't. "The car stalled. No idea why. Then a power pole fell on it. So, basically, no more van."

"The thing was a burned husk by the time I got there," Casey added. "You are all really lucky you got out."

I nodded. "Very."

Mom's eyes widened, but she must have caught the significance of what had happened and didn't immediately pepper us with questions.

Robby hooked his arm in Casey's and led her away, still whispering.

Geraint shook his head.

"Wait, are they together?" Mom frowned.

"I have no idea what's going to happen with that. Casey doesn't know what she's getting into, but Robby has been instructed that drastic things will happen if he breaks her heart."

"Well, that's interesting." Mom watched as the pair headed toward the cabins they were both living in.

"Let's get Nic inside," I said and headed for the house.

As soon as he was out of sight of anyone who didn't already know he was a shadowy Nightmare prince, he stepped into the nearest shadow and vanished, leaving me and Geraint alone with Mom.

"Geraint, are you all right? You're covered in bruises."

"Oh," we both said in unison. I was certain Geraint hadn't forgotten, but I had.

"I'm fine."

"You certainly don't look fine."

My knight shrugged. "I heal fast. The clown beat us all up some, but we're okay."

"Clown?" Mom's eyebrows rose.

"Maybe we should wait until Dad's here so we don't have to repeat ourselves?"

"All right, Ember," Mom said, and stopped asking questions.

We rejoined Nic just inside the door and headed for the kitchen. I, at least, was starving and thirsty.

***

"Conveniently," Robby said a few hours later. "There is an art gala at the museum in a few days, and I imagine I can get us an invitation to perform if we don't already have one." We had all crowded into my bedroom.

"What good does that do?" Dad asked. He leaned against the wall.

We'd filled both my parents in on what had happened. Now we were trying to figure out what to do with the information we'd gotten.

"Well, the bad guys apparently don't know why we were at the museum, and they don't know where Dio is. So, we need another excuse to go back to the museum that won't make it seem like we're looking for something there. Then we can liberate that rather priceless artifact from the display while we're there." Robby had perched on my sturdy dresser.

"How are we going to do that?" I frowned, squirming on my bed, uncomfortable with the suggestion. Geraint, sitting next to me, put his hand on my leg.

"Our shadowy prince is more than capable of stealing back Dio's essence," Robby explained.

I glanced at Nic, and he nodded, though his brow was furrowed as if troubled, and I caught a hint of unease through our bond. The rocking chair creaked as he pushed it back and forth while he thought.

"You and Geraint and I will do our normal routine, and if necessary, provide a distraction. Prince Nic will take care of getting Dio's essence back. Simple." Robby grinned.

"You jinxed us," I pointed out. "You know that, right?"

The jester inclined his head. "Perhaps."

I groaned. "This is crazy."

"What do we do about Dio?" Geraint asked once we'd had a minute to contemplate Robby's suggestions.

"Once we have his essence, we'll have to work quickly to get it back to him. Then we must try to find a way back to Dream," Robby said. "If nothing else, Dio needs to return, but also, we must find Baz."

"You think you know where he is?" I thought that was what Nic had said.

Robby shook his head. "I believe I know where to look, but there are still many options available to us. I suspect they've hidden him away in a corrupted dream, but which one, I don't know."

"How many are there?" I wrung my hands.

"Countless numbers of them, princess. Don't despair, we will find him." Robby sounded certain.

How could he be so sure? This is an impossible task.

Geraint put his arm around my waist and tugged me against his side. "It will work out, Spark."

I clenched my jaw but didn't argue. I'd probably spent as much time in Nightmare as Geraint had at this point. How could he possibly have any idea that it would work out? Mood souring further, I tried not to take it out on my friends.

When no one had any other questions, Robby pulled out his phone and scanned through his emails. "Your reputation proceeds you, princess. We have an invitation to perform. I'll accept with an apology on the late reply."

At my nod, he got up and left the room, phone to his ear.

"You all be careful," Mom said, twisting her hands together. Dad put an arm around her shoulders.

"Yeah, we will be."

My phone rang with Ash's tone, interrupting anything else I might say.

"Hey, Ash," I answered.

"Spark, what's up? You called?"

"Oh, right. Van trouble. We're home now, though."

"Trouble, huh? I'm on my way."

"Ash, you've got work," I protested.

"Nonsense. I cleared all my cases up for a bit. I was on vacation after today for a couple of weeks, anyway."

"Weren't you going to spend that time with your fiancé?"

"She had a family thing come up. I was going to join her, but I'm allowed to also have a family thing come up. No arguments. I'll be there in a couple of hours. You can fill me in, I'll help for a few days, and then future-wifey and I will go hang out on a beach."

"That sounds amazing," I said, thinking of the beach.

"Glad you like my plan. See you in a few. Love you, Spark." Ash hung up before I could correct her.

"Maybe you can talk her into performing with you at the fundraiser," Mom said. "The two of you haven't been in a lyra together in a long time. I'm sure the audience would love that."

"That's tomorrow, isn't it?"

Mom grinned. "Plenty of time to practice."

I laughed. "Sure it is."

The thing was, Ash and I could pull out a lyra performance with little preparation. We'd done it for years. So maybe Mom was right.

"In fact, you two should go in cold if Ash agrees. I know how to spin it to the crowd."

"Okay," I reluctantly agreed. She was totally going to turn it into a comedy show. She'd done it to us before. It wasn't my favorite, but we'd have fun, regardless.

CHAPTER 6

Geraint

"Knight." Ash punched me in the shoulder, not knowing that my arm was covered in bruises from a fight with a possessed mummy. At least she hadn't hit the open wounds on my other arm. Fortunately, I healed quickly or the performances tonight and, in a few days, would have been impossible.

"Hi, Ash." I tried to hide the wince.

She frowned. "What's wrong?"

"Just a little beat up from the museum."

She chuckled. "Not a sentence I ever expected to hear anyone utter, and I've heard some doozies in my career."

"I imagine you have." I watched as Robby taught Nic how to set up the school's portable aerial rig. Ember's dad supervised, occasionally lending a hand or explaining some aspect of the apparatus to the Nightmare prince.

"The three of you working out?" Her voice softened.

"Honestly, better than I had expected."

"I still can't believe you kept the whole Dream thing from us." She mock glared at me.

I cast my gaze at the floor and shrugged. "I would have told you if I could have."

"I know." Her voice sounded light and unconcerned. "So, how beat up are you?"

"If I didn't heal fast, I wouldn't be performing for a few weeks," I admitted. If I were honest with myself, today wasn't the best idea, but I'd wrap the cuts in case we broke them open—okay, when they broke open—so I wouldn't bleed everywhere, and I was wearing a dark long-sleeved shirt. We'd adjusted a few of the moves, giving Ember most of the "base" positions. She could hold my weight long enough to work our way through our time on stage. Nic had promised to keep a close eye on us in case my grip gave out. I don't think I would have agreed to perform if he hadn't been there to back us up. Ember had also agreed to the risk. If we made it through today without me dropping her or myself, we'd have to practice with Nic. I didn't want Ember to ever be afraid to be in the silks again.

She nodded. "I'll refrain from punching you for at least a few days then."

I grinned at Ash. "Thanks. So, you and Ember are resurrecting your comedy lyra routine?"

Ash shrugged. "I guess. I think we'd probably be okay without all the clowning around. We know our stuff and we have several relatively simple acts we could do in our sleep that still look impressive."

I winced again at the clown reference.

"Sorry, sorry." Ash shook her head and turned her attention over to Robby. Casey had shown up and was helping him.

"She has no idea, does she?"

I laughed. "Nope."

"I'll kill him if he hurts her."

"She does have a history of falling fast, then burning out quickly. At least as she's told it after a few drinks. I'm not worried about Casey's feelings so much as her actual safety. We've been attacked a few times now, and I'd hate to see her caught up in all of this."

"Crazy stuff." Ash cast her gaze over the auditorium.

This was a show we did every year. A benefit for the local underprivileged children to have access to extracurricular activities they might not otherwise be able to afford, one of them being the circus school Ember's parents ran. The money went into a scholarship fund and parents applied for different camps or experiences for their kids. The show itself had a minimal cost per ticket so anyone could attend and hopefully kids would get an idea of different activities they might want to try. Donations from the sponsors were the main source of income for the scholarship fund.

Ember entered the auditorium, and I focused on her as she came over to us.

Ash smirked. "Ember has entered the building."

"Your back is to the entrance," I pointed out. "It could be anyone."

"Knight, there's only one person who gets that look from you, and it's Spark."

"Point." I couldn't even begin to describe what Ember meant to me, but it didn't surprise me that my love for my spark showed in my expression.

Moments later, Ember came up to my side, putting her arm around my waist and tucking herself against me.

"Hey," she said.

"We were talking about our act," Ash said.

Ember smiled, shaking her head in resignation. "Yeah. I dug out my colorful leotard. It'll have to be enough. I don't think I can do the full clown makeup right now."

"No kidding," Ash agreed. "We should get ready though. We're the warmup act."

Ember stood on her toes, and I leaned down to kiss her, still astounded that I hadn't had to give her up. I thought I had been prepared for that eventuality, but as the years progressed and no one turned up from Nightmare to collect their princess, it got harder and harder to imagine not having her in my life. Ember had made it completely clear she wouldn't accept the princes without them accepting me. Nic accepted it. I had no idea if the other two would, but I doubted they'd be as understanding as the shadow prince.

"Geraint," Ember's mom called from the table at the front of the auditorium where the school's info was prominently displayed. "Can you help me with this?"

I hurried to her side. "Of course."

***

I shifted on the hard metal seat and stared at the stage, unaccustomed to this view. Normally, if I got to watch the acts, it was from backstage or on a monitor. Ember and I had plenty of time between her opening act and our closing performance and, for once, I wanted to watch from the audience.

Nic lurked in the shadows, and Robby would be stationed to work the lift on the lyra so it could raise and lower for this act.

Ember's mother came out on stage.

"Hello, everyone!" Her voice echoed around the room, carried over the mic she wore.

The full audience quieted while she introduced the school and told everyone what they did and the classes they provided.

I tuned her out, alert for trouble, but also focused on the stage. Nic was also on guard duty until Ember and I went on later. Then he would focus on us, and Robby would watch for trouble.

Finally, she introduced Ember and Ash.

Ember wandered out on stage as if lost, her bright leotard showing up brilliantly against the black curtains.

She held her hand over her eyes, shielding them from the bright stage lighting, and peered around, pretending that she was trying to figure out where she was.

While she looked out into the crowd, Robby lowered the lyra. Ash sat perched inside the hoop, feet crossed at the ankles. She wore a blue and pink leotard that showed off her full sleeve tattoos on her arms and her short hair was spiked up with gel.

Ash did a quick roll through the middle of her hoop, then hung from a knee and one hand, reaching the other toward Ember.

My spark still stared out over the crowd, peering around and acting confused.

Ash did another quick flashy display of rolls and poses in an attempt to get Ember's attention. When that didn't work, she dropped out of the lyra, put her hands on her hips and stalked over to the other woman.

Ember jumped when Ash put her hand on Spark's shoulder. She spun around and stared at Ash and threw her hands out, showing surprise at Ash's seemingly sudden appearance.

The music, quiet and instrumental and barely noticeable, now struck a stronger chord and a lively tune. Ash grabbed Ember's hand and pranced back toward the lyra. She placed Ember's hand on the bottom bar and gestured for Ember to get in.

Ember vehemently shook her head.

That was Robby's cue to lift the hoop into the air, with Ember dangling by one arm. Her eyes went wide, and she grabbed with the other hand as her feet left the ground.

She acted terrified, looking this way and that as she dangled above the stage and kicked her feet. Ash shook her head, grabbed Ember's foot, and danced around, spinning her cousin. She took ahold of Ember's ankles and hung there, spinning both of them as Robby lifted the pair higher.

After a few seconds, Ash spread her legs out, slowing their spin, and they descended until her feet were on the ground. She stopped Ember's rotations and skipped backward, holding both arms out to Ember with a big smile on her face, acting like she expected Ember to be happy.

Spark shook her head, took one hand from the lyra, and pointed toward the ground.

Ash put her hands on her hips and stomped a foot, pouting.

I chuckled at the play. They had another act that was similar but a bit more comedic that involved an announcer. I liked this one better though, and Ember did, too. I wasn't sure what Ash's opinion was, but she pranced around on stage like a champ while she tried to convince Ember that the lyra was fun. Ash's normal gait was more of a prowl than a prance, but the pair had developed this routine for kids' shows.

Robby finally set Ember down and Ash climbed back into the hoop, putting on an impressive display of spins and drops and poses while she showcased the lyra. All the while, Ember stood back, acting afraid.

When Ash descended from the hoop this time, she dragged Ember back over, but instead of throwing her into it, she mimed showing Ember some basic entrances and moves.

Ember reluctantly caved, letting Ash guide her through what would be a beginning lesson for a new student.

Ash clapped at Ember's first pose in the hoop. Slowly, Ember upped the difficulty of her movements until the song really picked up its pace. Then she leaned out of the hoop, much as Ash had at the beginning of their piece, and held out her hand.

Ash joined her in the hoop, and they posed as they spun, twisting through the various shapes together and making some completely fantastic poses, still in the very family friendly range. They had a couple of acts that would have been suitable for our last contract that had occasionally made me wonder how open Ash was to the idea of a threesome. Not that I'd ever suggested it.

The music came to its climax, and the cousins lowered themselves out of the lyra, hugged, clasped hands, and skipped off stage together.

The crowd cheered and the two women came back out on stage to take their bows before Ember's mom went into an introduction of the next act.

I stood and slipped out of the crowd, heading out of the room and toward the backstage area.

Ember and Ash were giggling like teens in the green room when I found them a few minutes later.

"Nicely done," I said, pulling Ember into a tight hug before punching Ash lightly on the arm. She caught herself before she made contact with my arm in her return punch.

"I'll save them up," Ash said with a wink.

"I'll hold you to it," I replied.

CHAPTER 7

Ember

Robby joined us, our act being the only one that required the lift. Casey got up from where she stretched and came over to the jester's side. He put his arm around her waist.

Well, okay then. I supposed it was as official as it could be at this point. I was in no position to judge her taste in men. I hoped we weren't putting her in danger.

"Where's Nic?" Casey asked.

"Lurking in the shadows," I replied.

Casey frowned. "Why?"

"He likes them," Robby said gently.

"Oh. Hey, Ember, I was wondering if I could go to the gala at the museum with you?" Casey twisted her hands as if nervous. "I think it would be a great way to get my name out there a little more."

Shit. There was no way I could say no and not offend her, but how could I say yes?

"Of course you can," Robby said. "We'll make your act meld in with theirs."

I stared at the jester. *"What are you doing?"* I mouthed behind her back.

He shrugged and planted a kiss on Casey's forehead.

"Ember, seriously, only if you don't mind. I'm not, like, trying to use Robby to get in on your business."

"Casey, you're more than welcome to perform with us. You're one of the most talented lyrists I've met, and I have no problem if you use your connections for evil." I elbowed Robby playfully. "He'll have to figure out the logistics, though. I'm not doing it." I hoped he got my meaning.

Robby nodded, and I supposed that was that.

"I'll come along, as well," Ash said. "If you're adding to your performance, you might need more support crew, and Nic isn't completely trained yet."

"Sounds great. Is future-wifey free yet? I bet we could get her a ticket." I was seriously going to kill Robby later. What on earth was he thinking? At least Ash understood that things were out of the ordinary and dangerous.

Ash shook her head. "Not for a couple more days."

"Bummer," I replied.

"Spark," Geraint said. "Let's go warm up."

I let my knight pull me away from the conversation and into our own corner. Wordlessly, we fell into our pre-show routine. I was already warmed up, but more stretching never hurt anything.

Completely in sync with each other, we moved through our warmup. I felt my breathing slow and my nerves calm. This was familiar. This was an activity I loved, and I was doing it with people I loved.

We stood, and Geraint pulled me into his arms.

"I love you, Spark," he murmured. "I love doing this with you."

My heart swelled near to bursting with his words, and I melted into his embrace. "I love you, Knight."

"Remember, I'm still torn up. Don't hesitate to use your shadows to hold on to me if you feel my grip waver. Prince Nic will spot us, too. I'll never drop you on purpose."

"I know," I assured him. "And I'm ready. Are you sure you want to do this? I can go on alone. They'll understand."

"This is a good time to practice using Nic as backup, just in case we have to do this again next week for the gala, or in the future. It could be a useful skill to develop, so we can practice now. Just be aware that my grip might give out."

"Okay." I bit my lower lip. "Geraint, I don't want to hurt you worse than you already are. Really, we can practice some other time."

"It's all right, Spark. This is a simple routine."

A little uneasy about the idea, but trusting both Geraint and Nic, I nodded. "Okay, Geraint. We'll do it, but if at any point it's too much, signal for floor work and I'll do the rest of the aerial."

"Deal."

Normally, I'd never agree to go up with a partner who wasn't positive he could keep a hold of me, but Nic would be there, and Geraint was right, this could be a useful skill in the future.

We spent the rest of the time before our performance discussing contingency plans for the routine. Confident we had a reasonable plan, I tracked Nic down. He lurked in the small alcove Robby had used to run our lift. He could see us both from there and from any of the shadows that lurked in the curtains. We'd be fine.

"Hey," I whispered.

"Hi, Spark."

"You ready?"

He nodded, his features shifting in and out of shadow for a moment before he settled.

"Is it getting easier to hold yourself steady?"

"Yes. Though I used to do it all the time as a child, so it shouldn't be as difficult as it has been."

"Some things are easier when you're younger, regardless." I stepped forward, putting my hand on his chest. "We have more energy when we're younger."

Nic chuckled. "That is very true."

I pressed my lips to his for a quick kiss. "Don't drop me."

"Your knight will keep you safe, and I'll make sure his grip is sure." He kissed me back, and then it was time for me to join Geraint and head for the stage.

Mom introduced us, and the music struck up.

Our floor work went as normal, fluid, graceful, grips sure and strong, but my knight's expression looked pinched, and I knew he was in pain.

He took to the air in the straps. His movements were flawless, but not as graceful as normal. I doubted anyone would notice unless they were well familiar with our abilities.

When it was time, I let Geraint take my hand. His grip was sure, but I felt tendrils of shadow essence wrap around us all the same. Even Geraint looked a little relieved as Nic supported us.

Halfway through our duet, I felt Geraint's muscles tremble. My arm slid through his momentarily, but Nic tightened his grip on the two of us. I didn't panic. Geraint didn't fall. My prince's help let us get through the rest of the aerial act with grace. Though I didn't have much concentration to chase the idea, the shadowy assistance gave me some thoughts about ways we might be able to apply this sort of trick in Nightmare. Especially if I got control of my own shadow powers.

We came down for the floor routine, bowed, and hurried backstage. I kept my arm around Geraint's waist, and he leaned against me.

"That was harder than it should have been," he admitted.

Nic and Robby joined us.

"Thank you, Nic," I murmured as Casey came over.

"Geraint, you all right?" she asked before Nic could reply to my whispered thanks.

Right, so she was pretty familiar with our acts. She would have noticed. My knight straightened, taking his weight from my shoulders.

"Yes, Casey. Thank you."

She frowned but didn't question him further. Robby led her off, and I helped Geraint to a chair.

"Knight," I said.

"I'm okay, Spark. I just need some rest. I think I'll take the week off." He grinned.

"Yeah, good call." I sat down next to him and stretched my legs out in front of me. "Nic, what's next?"

"We have to prepare for the gala next week. After that, we have to get back to Dream."

"Right. How?"

The prince tilted his head and shrugged. "That is the question, isn't it?"

***

Our gear and all of us wouldn't fit in one vehicle, so Robby drove Casey and our gear in one of the school vans, and Ash drove me, Nic, and Geraint in her SUV.

"How are we going to get the gem?" I asked again.

"We don't know, Spark," Geraint replied from the passenger seat.

"I'll have to see how it goes when we get there," Nic said. "We didn't have time to study the situation before, and returning would not have been wise."

"But we need a plan."

"Ember." Nic put his hand over mine and wrapped tendrils of shadow around me. My heart sped, and not from fear, as I remembered last night when he'd had me tangled up in his shadows. The way they'd caressed my body, their coolness contrasting with my heat and the warmth from Nic's hands. I remembered how good it felt when he slipped those tentacles of shadow up inside me, curling them around, expertly hitting all the best spots. Heat gathered between my legs, and I almost had an orgasm from the memory.

"Luv," Nic continued. "It'll be okay. You and Geraint, Robby and Ash, have a plan. I don't have to worry about getting captured by mortal authorities. I just have to get the essence out."

"So, yeah, actually you do, because they might have camera footage of us together when we were there last. If they do, then they could connect all of us, and I'm not ready to abandon the conscious realm completely." The camera thing hadn't occurred to me until now.

Nic pursed his lips and didn't reply for a few minutes. "I won't be seen or caught," he eventually promised.

"Sure. Fine. I'll stop. So, what are we going to do about Casey?"

Nic shrugged. "Robby assures me he has his love life under control."

I snorted.

"Let's try to keep her out of danger," Geraint suggested. "Otherwise, I think she's on her own with Robby. He's not an asshole, at least."

Thinking back to my chocolate-covered expresso beans, I grumbled. "I beg to differ."

Nic ran his hand up my leg, tendrils of shadow tightening around my ankles. I bit my lower lip and tried not to react.

Ash glanced at us in the rearview mirror, arching an eyebrow. "Do you two need to get a room?"

Geraint glanced back at us, chuckling in amusement.

"No," Nic replied.

"Maybe yes?" I protested.

Ash laughed.

Despite Nic's denial, the tentacles of shadow continued to crawl up my legs, squeezing gently but firmly, slipping between my legs, and teasing me.

"You're no good at poker faces, Ember," Ash said.

"Hey, it's not my fault Nic is feeling handsy," I muttered, cheeks heating.

Nic held up his hands, as if trying to prove his innocence, though he had an amused smirk on his face.

"I know your tricks, shadow boy," Ash stated.

"She looked bored," the prince said. The shadows slowly withdrew, leaving aching desire in their absence.

I pouted. "Damn it."

"Nic, there are three princes of Nightmare and three princesses of Dream?" Ash asked.

"Yes. Currently. There are always three and three, but they are not always composed of three princes and three princesses. It is simply even this time. Our Queen was once a Nightmare princess, and our King was of Dream. Though even this ruling structure has mutated over time as humans change the way they view things. It's possible next time the energies cycle through to recreate the caretakers of Dream, we will have a different system."

"Hey, so, are there spaceships and aliens and like ray guns and stuff in Dream?" Ash glanced at Nic for a moment before turning her attention back to the road.

"Yes."

"Whoa," I said. "Wait, really?"

"Anything humans have ever dreamed exists in the dream realm. It's merely a matter of how common and strong the dreams are as to how prominently and frequently they occur. Aliens, like cryptids and the prettier types of vampires and whatnot, live within the boundaries.

Nightmares and more pleasurable dreams support them. Though, are they truly alien if they're created by human thoughts?"

Ash opened her mouth to argue, tilted her head, then snapped her mouth shut again. "That's a deeper question of philosophy than I care to think about the day before I help commit a crime."

"Is it really a crime if we're retrieving an object that belongs to someone else?" Nic's lips twitched up into a smile.

"I suppose if we want to go with that argument, the museums should start returning a lot of things to their former owners." Ash shook her head.

The prince nodded. "Likely."

"I would very much like to go for a ride in a spaceship, even if it's an imaginary one," Ash mused.

"You would become dreambound if you entered Dream," Nic cautioned.

"Yeah, I know." Ash sighed. "Still—"

"I can influence your dreams if you would like a particularly vivid one tonight," Nic said.

"Can you do it without it turning into a nightmare?" Ash glanced at the prince. "You know, since nightmares are your thing and all?"

"Ahh, point. I can ask Robby. I believe jesters have that power as well."

"I still can't believe you assholes kept this from us," Ash grumbled and sent a mock glare at Geraint.

He didn't rise to the bait, shrugging instead. "Like I said, if I could have told you, I would have."

"I know." Ash pushed out her lip in a fake pout. "So, what other interesting things can we talk about?"

"How do dreams end up in the conscious realm other than going through arches? We've got to figure out how to get back. Maybe talking about that will spark an idea."

This part of our plan had me more worried than anything else at the moment. Dio needed to get home, and we had no idea how to accomplish it. Robby had managed to get out the traditional way, but unless we found Bloody Mary, we weren't going to get back through a mirror.

"There are places where the boundaries between the conscious realm and Dream are weaker. Places where a great deal of disturbance has happened in the past, for example, haunted locations."

"Wait, ghosts aren't real?" Ash interrupted.

Nic shrugged. "I'm not sure I'm the best authority on what is real and what isn't. My entire world is formed from imagination, after all. However, some ghosts are formed from people's dream energy. Not all."

"Okay," Ash said.

"Yes, so, as I was saying—"

"Sorry," Ash mumbled.

Nic chuckled. "I'm not mad. In any case, the power of enough belief can draw dream energy through to the conscious realm and form it. Sometimes it pulls creatures through, sometimes it simply takes energy that has already leaked through and gives it shape. As I told Ember, there's a fair chance the clown and the vampires we faced had never even been to Dream.

"We usually recruit more powerful and loyal dreams to help keep these rogue dreams in check. That is normally the entire purpose of the guards and royalty, if you want to call us that, in the Dream realm. Keeping rogue dreams from getting too disruptive or powerful in the conscious realm. Things are out of balance since we haven't been able to perform our duties in the last ten years or so."

We fell silent, contemplating Nic's words. Ash finally turned the radio up a little, and I stared out the window, one hand in Nic's. We weren't far from the main part of Pittsburg, and the suburbs had crowded out the cornfields.

The school van that Robby drove was right in front of us. So far, the trip had gone without incident. Hopefully that continued, but I wasn't going to hold my breath.

I let my mind wander while Ash drove, considering what Nic had said. Weakness in the boundaries.

"Is there a way to tell where the weaknesses are?" I asked after a lengthy silence. "And is it something we can get through?"

"Fully formed dreams getting through the weak points are very rare. I don't know if that is a pathway we can utilize for us to travel. It's worth looking into, but it's also possible we could do enough damage to tear the barrier and let more through."

"If we desperately have to get Dio back to Dream, we may not have a choice," I pointed out.

Nic took a breath and nodded. "I am not sure it will work."

"You also weren't sure I could repair the arch."

My prince gave me a fond smile. "I knew you could do it. I just wasn't sure if you would be able to figure it out under the circumstances. I remembered from our childhood that the best way to motivate you was to act like I didn't think you could accomplish something."

I stuck out my tongue and folded my arms across my chest.

Ash, Geraint, and Nic all laughed at me.

"Assholes," I muttered.

"So, if we will it hard enough, we could make unicorns and stuff in these weak areas?" Ash asked innocently.

"Potentially. I would advise against trying, however."
"Why?"

"Unicorns tend to be very, uh, stabby," Nic answered.

"They do essentially have giant swords on their foreheads," Geraint pointed out.

"Yes, and most of them are mares," Nic said. "Once you win them over, they're yours for eternity, but winning them over can be extremely difficult, and often results in stab wounds."

"Bummer," Ash muttered. "Always wanted a unicorn."

"Thought you wanted a vampire," I kidded.

"Yeah, well, future-wifey would have to agree at this point." Ash glanced at the GPS. "All right, I have to focus. I think we're close to our exit."

Half-formed ideas churning in my mind, I stared out the window as the buildings changed from suburban to urban. Maybe I could use my powers of creation to make a different type of arch?

Those thoughts carried me until we pulled into the parking garage for our hotel. Nic stayed with the van while those of us with actual identification went through the check-in process. Then we came back, grabbed our bags, and headed for our rooms. Ash had her own. Robby and Casey shared, and Nic, Geraint, and I took another.

As Robby would handle all the check-in details for the performance, the rest of us had time on our hands. I glanced at the king-sized bed and my mates and grinned. "Yes?"

Geraint already knew what I was thinking from long years together. He inclined his head, a mischievous glint in his eyes. It took Nic a moment longer for his eyebrows to raise and a soft smile to flit across his lips.

"If you like," Nic replied.

"Duh." I spun around and flopped onto the bed. "If you are both still okay with group activities, after the first time."

Geraint and Nic traded a glance before both nodded. "Yes, Spark, it's fine with us."

"Great!" I kicked off my shoes and shed my clothing in record time, leaving the guys staring at me with a mixture of hunger and surprise lighting up their eyes and curling their lips.

It didn't take long for Geraint to pull his shirt off, and I licked my lips as those powerful muscles rippled with his movement. I couldn't wait to run my tongue over those ridges and trace those valleys until they led me to his delicious cock.

"You might stretch a little," Geraint suggested with a wink before going over to the bed and pulling the covers down.

I quickly did a few warmups, being sure to stick my butt in the air enticingly in Nic's direction. He opened his mouth, tongue wetting his lips. I didn't always stretch before sex, but the night before a performance was a crappy time to pull a muscle so I did what I was told.

Geraint lay down on the bed and gestured for me to join him.

I walked up onto the bed and slid into a center split right over his face. He caught my hips with the ease of long practice and brought me where he wanted me.

"Join us," I said to Nic.

He melted into shadow, swirling across the room then solidifying on the bed in front of me positioned on his knees. Geraint applied his talented tongue to my clit while Nic cradled my cheeks with his hands and pressed his lips to mine.

They both thoroughly kissed me until I was trembling, each stroke of Geraint's tongue bringing me closer and closer to climax, while Nic shared his love and passion as we kissed.

"Oh, just like that," I gasped, interrupting my kiss with Nic as pressure coiled in my core before exploding through me.

"How would you like to have us?" Nic asked, his hands trembling on my cheeks as he looked me right in the eye.

Warm tingles of happiness curled through me at the way he asked how I wanted them. This seriously was the best. I'd never thought it could be any better than what Geraint had given me for years, his love, devotion, and skills were everything I needed, but adding Nic into our mix had taken things to an entirely new level I'd never known could exist. That they both loved me and were willing to share me, at the same time even, warmed me even further.

"Both at once. If you're okay with that?" I glanced at Nic. I'd let them decide how exactly they would accomplish that.

"I'm happy to try anything with you at least once," Nic replied with a pleased smile.

I looked down at Geraint beneath me.

"Ride me," he said, his face slick with my juices and a happy light in his eyes. "Nic can take you from behind."

"Ahh, which hole am I to take you in? I've seen a lot of dreams, so I'd like to be clear which you are expecting."

"Mmmm, I could go for either," I replied, pretty sure my pussy was up to the task of taking both if they were willing.

"Just slide on in with me, if you like," Geraint said. "Never tried it before, but I don't have any objections."

"Very well," Nic answered.

"You're always welcome to say no," I insisted.

"I will tell you if I'm uncomfortable or not enjoying myself," Nic said. "You do the same. Until then, let's try it." He brushed a strand of hair out of my eyes.

I grinned and slid down Geraint's chest, the breeze from the ceiling fan cooling the sweat on my over sensitive skin and making me shiver at the touch of the moving air.

He groaned as I squeezed with my thighs before reaching back and finding his hard cock. I ran my fingers over his velvety length, looking forward to being stuffed incredibly full.

Geraint hissed out a breath, his fingers tightening on my hips. Knowing I would impale myself after I played, he shut his eyes in anticipation.

I wanted to tease him, to wait, but my desire to be crammed full of cock won out over my patience, and I seated myself on him, crying out as I took him to the root in one motion.

"Gods, that feels so good." I shut my eyes and ran my hand down my stomach to my stretched pussy, playing with my clit.

"No place I'd rather be, Spark," Geraint replied.

Nic shifted around until he was behind me, also straddling Geraint's legs. I leaned forward so I lay on my knight's chest. Geraint dug his fingers into my sides and Nic ran his hands lightly over my ass.

"Ready?"

"Stuff me, please," I said, a little nervous but very excited to see how this was going to go.

Nic chuckled, running his cock against my soaked thighs for some lubricant before pushing into my opening.

"Oh, holy shit," I breathed as he pushed into me, his cock sliding along Geraint's and pressing into me.

He paused. "Too much?"

For a moment it was too much, but then my body adjusted. "Keep going."

He did, sliding in until he was fully seated.

"Wow," I said. Stuffed was right. I felt like I might burst, but at the same time, I was so full they were hitting every spot just right.

"How is it for you two?"

"Deliciously tight," Geraint said with a groan.

"Yes," Nic answered, voice heavy with lust.

"Great, try moving."

They did, and I saw stars. It took them a few tries to get a rhythm down, but I didn't even mind, just riding the wave of ecstasy that was building in my pussy and spreading to my extremities. Everything tingled. It was as if their combined cocks were touching me everywhere, from the tips of my toes and building a heated fire through my core and up into my chest as my two lovers wrecked me completely.

I swore happily as they picked up speed, and my first orgasm caught me by surprise.

"Oh, this is amazing."

"Not going to last long," Geraint said through gritted teeth.

"Understandable," I squeaked out just as my body shattered again. My vision blackened at the edges my limbs turned to jelly.

They managed to roll me through one more powerful release before both of them came, one right after another.

Nic collapsed onto my back, putting me in the middle of a man-candy sandwich. Neither pulled out, and my body still shuddered with the aftereffects of riding both of them at once.

We lay there, recovering, for I didn't even know how long. They both softened inside me before pulling out.

"That was intense," I finally said. My stomach muscles felt like I'd done a huge core day, and my pussy felt deliciously used.

"Intense and pleasurable," Nic said.

Geraint nodded, perhaps not capable of forming words yet.

I didn't even have the energy to try and talk them into after sex, shower sex. While I contemplated that injustice, I drifted off to sleep.

CHAPTER 8

Ember

Memories

I dodged the snowball, giggling as it splattered into the tree instead of my chest.

"Missed me!"

Dio shook his fist at me, then bent over to grab more snow. I took off into the forest where the snow wasn't as deep, trying to put distance between us. Nic stepped out from behind one of the trees and tackled me.

"Hey!" I fell to the ground, laughing and fishing up a small bit of snow and throwing it at his face.

He fell back with a playful yelp.

I scrambled to my feet and took off, but Dio had time to catch up. He loved tag more than anything, and it didn't take much for one of our games to turn to chase.

Baz came in from the other side, nailing both Nic and Dio in the face with snow. They were pretty brutal with each other, but they tended to avoid face shots with me. I appreciated it.

A rock pile blocked my path. Instead of going around, I decided to go over. The rocks were dry enough, and I thought the boys still roughhoused from the laughing and shouting behind me.

We were in a part of the forest I didn't know as well, but I had my friends with me, so I'd be safe. I scrambled to the top, just as Dio came bounding up the rocks after me. He always made climbing seem so easy.

I backed away from the snowball still held in his hand. "Not fair!"

"Totally fair," he replied with a grin.

I took another step backward but met only air when I put my foot down. I had only a second to contemplate my mistake before I tumbled into the air.

"Nic!" Dio shouted.

I shrieked, heart racing, certain the hard stop at the end of the fall was going to break me.

My vision clouded, swirling with black smoke, and a cool, comforting blanket closed around me, slowing my fall, cushioning me until I landed gently at the bottom of a ravine I hadn't known was there.

I blinked, staring up at the three faces of my best friends. Nic seemed to swirl into existence out of shadows or some sort of smoke.

"What happened?"

"Nothing, Ember," Dio assured me. "Just a little slip."

"But—"

"You're fine. Just watch your step. Now forget this happened." Dio touched my forehead.

I blinked a few more times before my vision cleared completely. We stood in the snowy field. Something was weird about that, but I wasn't sure what.

The snowball in my face distracted me completely.

"Hey!"

"You're it!" Dio shouted.

"Jerk!" I grabbed a pile of snow and sprinted after my friend. They weren't supposed to hit me in the face.

CHAPTER 9

Ember

The slinky green dress I wore showed off my legs to their max effect, covered one shoulder, but left the one with my silks harlequin clown tattoo bare. Geraint's forest green suit paired well my sparkly attire, and I felt like a star as we wandered around the gathering with me on his arm. We both held champagne flutes to blend in, but we drank water. Even if we hadn't been part of a questionable heist, we wouldn't have had any alcohol until after we performed.

Nic lurked in the shadows, working on his plan to liberate Dio's essence. We had already erected our aerial rig and heavy red cloth shrouded it and the rest of the stage. The performances would start in a few hours. Until then, a string quartet played, and people moved amongst the displays. Like every other charity benefit we'd performed at, about half the people were genuinely interested in the artifacts and almost everyone was interested in being seen.

The elite spoke with us, but some inherent sense they had told them we weren't on their perceived level. Many of them recognized us from previous shows, or from the poster the museum had hastily put up when we'd accepted their invitation last week. We were fancy performers, but we were still the entertainment.

Little did they know I was the royalty of their dreams. Not that the title meant anything right now. The only thing I'd even remotely done to earn that title was save Nic's life after not-Baz had tried to drain him of essence and kill him.

Regardless, I didn't care what they thought, as long as they continued to donate their money and didn't use their considerable influence to block my progress. Geraint and I smiled and nodded at all the right places and floated from conversation to conversation so we could be seen.

Robby, with Casey on his arm, made his way through the crowd much like we did. He somehow charmed everyone in his path. Perhaps it was his jester skills, or maybe it was an inherent aspect of what and who he was. People liked me and Geraint. They loved Robby. I supposed we were lucky to have him, and I certainly didn't mind the effect he had on people.

"How much longer?" Geraint asked out of the corner of his mouth.

I glanced at my fancy wristwatch. "Another half an hour."

My knight sighed. "I used to enjoy this part a lot more."

Chuckling, I kept my stage smile plastered on my face. "Same here. At least we only do charity events a few times a year."

Geraint raised my hand to his lips and kissed it. "I can't decide if this is better or worse than pouring drinks."

"Just be thankful..." I trailed off, not wanting to jinx us.

"What?"

"Uh, I was going to say be thankful none of the bad guys are here, but I guess we don't know that. Do we?" I shuddered at my memories.

"Robby checked in with the librarian," Geraint said.

"Right. Badass ghost librarian says we're safe. I guess we'll have to trust her."

"I do."

"Yeah, so do I." She'd saved our butts, among other things.

Robby and Casey joined us before I could dwell on our last visit to this esteemed establishment.

"Are you two ready?" I asked.

"Yes." Casey beamed. "I'm so glad to be here. Thank you so much."

"Of course. Have you ever done one of these before?" I scanned the crowd uneasily but didn't see anything out of the ordinary.

"No."

"They're fun," I allowed.

"It's time to head backstage and prepare," Robby said.

We all threaded our way through the crowd, and it didn't take long before we made it to our green room area to change.

One of the folks in charge of the gala stepped inside and talked with Robby while Geraint, Casey, and I changed into our costumes and touched up our makeup.

After we were ready, we stretched and warmed up as best we could. Fortunately, Geraint was feeling much better, and neither of us thought he'd have a problem with the piece we'd chosen for tonight.

Casey kissed Robby before heading out to the stage to wait for her turn. She was the third act, and we were the closing one.

I arched an eyebrow.

Robby looked slightly abashed. "She's growing on me."

"She's in danger."

The jester nodded. "Yes. And I am still trying to think of what I can tell her about our absence when we go back to Dream."

"Better be something good."

"It is possible she'll tire of me before then. I still don't know how we're going to get home." Robby sighed.

"Well, I guess we'll figure it out." The idea of creating a new type of arch surfaced again. Nic had said I had the power of creation in the Dream realms. Maybe that meant I could do something about getting us back.

The music changed tempo as the performances started, interrupting my train of thought.

Geraint put his arm around me, and I leaned against his solid warmth. Robby spared us a glance I couldn't interpret before turning his attention to the stage.

The crowd applauded, and I centered myself, preparing mentally for our performance.

CHAPTER 10

Nic

Being back in the museum was not the most comfortable feeling after being attacked by the clown. Though I stuck to the shadows so I wouldn't be seen, I found myself looking over my shoulder. I was a prince of Nightmare. I shouldn't have to be afraid of anything. And maybe I wasn't afraid for myself. If I'd simply had to fight or get away the other day, it wouldn't have been an issue. I could fight a clown one-on-one and win. I'd done it once before. Not that it had been easy, but I'd done it. The fear wasn't for me, it was for Ember, and even Robby and Geraint. Maybe even Ash and Casey. I felt responsible for them, now that they were part of our group.

Shaking off the emotions and keeping my senses alert, I flitted from shadow to shadow. It didn't take long to make it to the display that housed Dio's essence. What had he been thinking? I hadn't even known it was possible to survive separating from your dream essence, but apparently, it was.

The guard from before was absent, the museum not open to the public today. I had no doubt that the camera and alarm systems would be present, but I could probably get around those. And if not, at least I wouldn't get caught, and I wouldn't be identifiable as anything but a shadowy blur.

99

Finding a deep shadow, I sent out tendrils of essence to explore, and settled in to study my target and wait for the right time. If I took it too soon, it could cause problems for the others, and we wanted to avoid that.

***

A couple of hours later, I heard the music change as the performances started. Guests had been wandering through regularly, many of them stopping to admire Dio's essence. The last of the observers left for the entertainment, and I got ready to make my move.

I did a quick check in the shadows and, to my surprise, noticed a new presence. This person strolled into the gem room once everyone else had cleared out.

A sharpness about her attitude set off alarms in my mind, but she wasn't from Dream, so I didn't suspect I was in any danger of discovery. Curious, I watched. She wore a silver dress with a long slit up the side, showing muscular legs. She opened her purse and slipped an object out.

I watched her go up to the case containing Dio's essence, point the long thin device at it, then somehow, she removed the gem, dropped it and the device in her purse, and left. Her actions were smooth and practiced. I stared, shocked.

What in the hell? Stunned, it took me a minute to react, and by then the woman had wandered out of the exhibit area. I slipped from the shadow I crouched in to another one with a better vantage point.

She looked over her shoulder, as if sensing a pursuer, though I was well shrouded.

After a moment, it became clear it wasn't me she was worried about. A man in a suit strode toward her, disbelief warring with anger on his face as he spied the woman.

She grinned, gave a quick wave, and dashed toward the stairs.

Feeling like I was on the set of a heist movie, I slipped into another shadow, not wanting to lose track of the woman who had casually taken Dio's essence. I needed to stop her, but Ember's worry about dealing with the authorities kept me from acting inside the museum. It might have been a mistake, but I didn't think I would lose track of her.

Adding to the heist movie feel, she casually pulled the fire alarm as she slipped out of the building, leaving the man in the suit fuming in her wake.

Torn between wanting to protect Ember and needing to follow the woman, I had to remind myself that she had Robby and her knight. Ember would be okay, and if we lost that essence, it might be impossible to find again.

I slipped into the shadows of the parking garage and trailed her until she hurriedly got into a non-descript sedan, again conscious of the likelihood of cameras. That would have been an excellent opportunity to relieve her of the gem, but she got the car in motion before I could slide into a shadow inside her vehicle, and I didn't want to spook her into an accident. The man with the suit was running now, and he reached a sportier car than the woman drove. I had half a mind to text Robby and make sure there wasn't some sort of movie filming going on at the same time as the gala.

She sped out of the parking garage, and the guy in the suit gave chase.

If her purse with Dio's essence hadn't been on her lap, the strap still over her shoulder, I would have taken it and slipped away.

Then it occurred to me I'd seen that man in the suit before. He'd toned down his powers to slip past the librarian, which is why I hadn't recognized him. Maybe this woman *was* working for Dream?

Either way, I didn't feel right leaving her at the mercy of the clown.

CHAPTER 11

Ember

The confusion and the panic of the fire alarm finally abated, and we were allowed back inside to retrieve our equipment.

Wondering how Nic was, I helped Robby tear down our rig. I didn't feel my connection to the prince as strongly as when he was close, and I wondered what that meant. Was he in trouble? Who had triggered the alarm? Surely Nic wouldn't have needed that kind of distraction.

As soon as we had the school van packed, Robby touched base with the gala organizer and then we headed back for the hotel, none of us speaking about Nic because of Casey's presence.

"Well, that was weird," Casey said once we were away.

"Very," I agreed.

"It's a bummer you and Knight didn't get a chance to perform."

"Yeah," I said. Though I was of mixed feelings about that. Part of me was disappointed, the other part of me was glad that we were done with that portion of the evening.

"Your performance was mesmerizing," Robby said to Casey.

She visibly melted at the jester's praise.

"Lay it on a little thicker, Robby," I said with a smile.

I caught Robby's lips quirking into his own smile in the rearview mirror.

"I'm not lying."

"I know. Casey is phenomenal with a lyra," I said.

"Thank you, Ember. That means a lot coming from you." Casey grinned at me.

"My dear, do you mind if I abandon you for a couple of hours this evening? Ember, Geraint, and I need to have a business meeting."

"Oh, not at all. There's a buffet calling my name. And remember, you're always welcome to tell me I can't tag along," she said. "I'm not trying to take advantage of you."

"Casey," I replied with as reassuring a voice as I could manage through my worry for Nic. "You're very welcome to travel with us. It might even make sense for us to join our acts more formally. We can see how the next few months go. Our meeting is just something we do every now and again. I'm sure Robby will fill you in on the pertinent details."

Casey twisted around in her seat, eyes wide. "Really?"

"Yeah, Casey. We think you're great."

"Wow, okay."

I just hoped we could keep her safe until things settled, because I did enjoy her company. We fell quiet, lost in our own thoughts, while Robby drove.

It didn't take long to reach the parking garage for our hotel. Robby found a spot, and we all piled out. Robby took the lead and Geraint fell behind, keeping the three of us women between them. I wasn't sure if Casey noticed, but Ash did. Fortunately, we made it to the elevator with no issues and crowded inside.

I hated being on edge like this. Robby scanned his key card, and the car went up to our floor. When we made it off the elevator with no incident, I took a deep breath. I wasn't sure why I'd been worried about that, but if the enemy could drop a power pole on our van, chances were, they could mess with the elevator, too. I wondered if Nic had gotten Dio's essence.

Ash made like she was heading to her room but gave me a quick look over her shoulder. She'd be back as soon as Casey was out of sight.

Robby gave the lyrist a steamy kiss while Geraint and I rolled our eyes, then we went into our room.

"Nic?" I called, already knowing he wasn't here.

"Where is our Nightmare Prince?" Robby asked.

"Uh." I spun in a circle until the connection between us strengthened. "That way."

Robby's eyebrows rose. Someone knocked on the door before he could ask me any other questions.

Geraint went to let Ash in.

"Okay, where's shadow boy?" She looked around.

"We're not sure." I hugged myself.

"They didn't, like, take him, did they?" Ash sank down into one of the chairs.

"I don't think so. He doesn't feel distressed, not that I'm very good at this. I just know he's not here, and he's getting farther away."

"I doubt Nic is in trouble. The real question is, why hasn't he simply slipped through the shadows to meet us here?" Robby replied. "If we need to go to him, I'm going to have to come up with a better excuse for Casey."

We all stared at Robby for a few seconds. "Why did you bring her?" I blurted.

The jester shrugged. "She asked nicely."

"Don't get me wrong. I really like Casey, and I meant everything I said earlier." I ran my hand through my hair and sighed. "I just don't want her getting hurt because she got tangled up in our mess. It's bad enough that Ash is in danger because of us."

105

My cousin shrugged, not acting concerned. "I'm happy to help."

Just then Nic stepped out of the shadows, interrupting anything else I might have to say on the matter.

"Did you get it?" I sprang to my feet and wrapped my prince in a hug.

"No."

"Why ever not?" Robby asked.

"Long story, which I'm about to tell." Nic launched into the story of the woman in the silver dress, the clown, and how they had interrupted his attempt to get Dio's essence.

"That's insane, but now we need to save her from the clown and get the essence?" I flopped back on the bed and stared at the ceiling. "Seriously?"

Nic patted my thigh. "Yes, luv. Seriously. I am not certain the clown has found the thief yet. If so, we simply have to confront her and escape before he finds her. I doubt he'll have much use for her if she doesn't have the essence.

"I wonder how the clown found out what we were after." I shuddered.

"Hard to say," Robby replied. "It's possible he or an agent of his returned to the museum and looked around until he figured it out. They obviously hid from the librarian, which limited their powers, but they still figured out why we were there."

"Do you think they've found Dio?" The thought made my blood run cold.

"Unlikely," Robby said.

"It won't matter if they find Dio if they get a hold of his essence," Nic said. "Destroying that will destroy Dio, eventually."

"So we're leaving?"

Nic twisted his lips. "It will take time for us to drive there. Robby and I will have to go."

"I'm going with you," I blurted. I scrambled to my feet and quickly stripped out of my leotard so I could change into more practical clothing, not caring that Robby was present. He'd seen me change on more than one occasion.

"Spark," Geraint said. "They need to use their powers to go."

"I have shadow powers, too," I replied stubbornly as I hastily got dressed in street clothing.

"If you can meld with the shadows enough to allow me to take you through them, you can come," Nic replied.

"You don't think I can do it." I bit my bottom lip and glared at him.

He smiled. "I'm hoping it takes you a little longer to figure it out, Spark. I don't want you in danger, but I also don't want you trying on your own to come after me and getting lost."

"That sounds unpleasant."

"Very. Perhaps worse than facing the clown." Nic sounded like he was trying to dissuade me.

"Spark—" Geraint sighed and shook his head. "I can't travel that way."

I sucked my lower lip into my mouth and chewed on it for a moment, tempted to remain behind. Did I want to face the clown? No. Did I think I could help? I actually didn't know. Why was I trying to go along, anyway?

"If you can figure out how to go through the shadows, you can support Prince Nic with your energy should we have to face the clown," Robby said. "It's not the worst idea to come along. It is unfortunate your knight can't join us."

Swallowing, I nodded agreement, rethinking my insistence that I dive into danger. No, if I could help Nic, I had to go.

Nic held out his hand once I finished dressing.

107

I quickly gave Geraint a kiss, hugged Ash, then accepted Nic's hand.

"Meld with the shadows, princess. We don't have a lot of time," Robby ordered.

Taking a deep breath and shutting my eyes, I called on my shadow powers. They were easier to access every time I touched them, but that didn't mean it was easy.

Still, I let my mind sink into the shadows, let them caress me, remembered what it felt like to be wrapped up in their cool embrace when Nic hid me in them, or wrapped me up with his shadowy tentacles. That thought brought a bit of heat to my cheeks. Then I gave myself over to the darkness, trusting Nic to keep a hold of me.

Someone sucked in a breath, and someone else swore, but their voices were muffled. I opened my eyes, but my vision had blurred. Everything was in black and white, but I couldn't make out details.

Nic still held my hand.

"Almost, princess," he whispered. "You can do it. Let go."

At first, I wasn't sure what he meant, but then I understood that I still grasped onto the solid world as an anchor. I had no idea how to give that up. Fear gripped me. If I let go, how would it change me? Could I really do this?

"I've got you, Ember," Nic whispered. "Let go. It'll be all right."

I couldn't do it. That solidness was everything I knew and understood about the world.

"Your highness, we'll have to leave her, and we must go," Robby said.

Fuck you, Robby, I thought, and let the shadows take me.

Panic trailed icy fingers through me, curling into my gut and making my insides feel liquid—except I didn't have insides. Or outsides. I no longer existed except as an expanding ball of panic in the cold nothing. *Had I screwed up? Was I dead?*

I was totally dead.

I've got you. Nic's voice echoed around me.

Was he dead, too?

The scattered wisps of shadows that felt most connected to me, pulled together and suddenly sight, weight, and all my other senses returned.

I reeled, body freaking the fuck out as it tried to adapt. Arms wrapped around my stomach and kept me from hitting the floor. I heaved once, but though my body cramped like I wanted to puke, I managed to keep the contents of my stomach down.

"Holy shit, Ember," Ash said. "You totally swirled into some sort of shadowy mist like shadow boy does. That was badass."

"Ohmygod." With Nic's help, I sank to my knees and planted my palms on the floor.

"Ember, maybe you should practice a few times before you try to travel through the shadows." Nic rubbed my back.

Geraint came to his knees next to me and touched my shoulder.

"Maybe," I reluctantly agreed. I was in no condition to help Nic like this.

"Don't be disappointed," Nic said. "For someone not born to the power, you did very well. It's disorientating to my regular senses every time I do it. I'm simply used to the sensation."

"Your regular senses?"

"Sight, smell, my sense of where I am in relation to the world," he explained.

"Oh, yeah, my equilibrium is all screwed up." The world was swimming around me.

"You have to learn to navigate and see with the shadows. I should have insisted you get comfortable looking through the shadows before you tried to join with them." He squeezed my shoulder.

"Right. Okay. At least I did it. You won't be able to fight the clown if you're having to deal with me puking my guts out, though, so I guess I'll have to stay here. Robby, you have your phone, right?"

"Yes, princess."

"Do me a favor and tell me where you're at, so if anything goes wrong, we have a point to search." I hated to think like that, but this was a clown we were talking about.

"I will," the jester assured me.

Nic kissed my forehead before straightening. "We will be back soon," he promised.

"I'll hold you to that." I almost changed my mind, wanting to go with Nic and make sure he stayed safe, but a wave of nausea washed through me. Yeah, there was no way.

Nic and Robby vanished.

"So, who's hungry?" Ash clapped her hands together.

I flipped her off.

CHAPTER 12

Nic

The woman in the silver dress was where I'd left her, a small hotel room on the border of the city. The room exited into the parking lot and her car was right outside her door. She'd changed, probably showered by her wet hair, and now looked like any other traveler wearing jeans and a band t-shirt.

I sensed a hint of Nightmare coming from the black bag she had sitting on the edge of the hotel bed. It still boggled my mind that this woman had stolen the gem at the same time I'd been after it. What were the odds?

She grabbed the bag and headed for the door. I swirled out of the shadows in front of her.

To the woman's credit, she yelped and reached for a gun instead of screaming. I kept the shadows close, shifting in and out of being in case she pulled the trigger.

"Who the hell are you?"

"You don't know?" I needed to know if she was involved with Dream or not.

She sneered at me. "If I wasn't stone cold sober, I'd think I was on some sort of bad trip."

I sensed Robby step from his version of the shadows behind her. I didn't look, not wanting to give him away. Letting shadows swirl around me, I became more monster than man, hundreds of tentacles reaching out like some sort of eldritch horror, shadows obscuring my features, letting my eyes shine in the lamplight.

The woman's hand shook, and she backed away, clutching the black bag with Dio's essence. The gun remained pointed in my direction despite her fear.

"Give it to me." Instead of holding out my hands, I snaked tentacles of shadow across the ground.

The thief whimpered.

"Clown," Robby hissed.

She spun at his voice.

The walls melted around us.

I snagged the bag with Dio's essence in it, using my shadows, and tossed it to Robby. "Go!"

Robby caught the bag, glanced between me and the thief, and vanished.

For her part, she'd spun back around and pointed the gun at me. I melted into the shadows completely, using my extra senses to keep my bearings as the clown warped reality.

He chuckled, walking through the closed door as if it didn't exist. The creature still wore his charcoal gray suit, and didn't look like a clown, but I knew his reflection would show his true nature.

The thief shrieked and pulled the trigger, aiming for the center of his chest. Bullets sped through the air, then slowed more and more until they hung suspended inches from impact. The creature laughed and plucked them from the air.

Were I a lesser man, I would have left her. I couldn't leave a mortal to the mercies of this brutal nightmare creature, though. It was part of my job to control these beings, regardless of how I felt about it.

White and gray lines swirled through the air, spinning, spiraling, making it hard to focus. The woman staggered, dropped her gun, and clutched her head.

I sent tendrils of shadow toward the clown. Though we weren't in Nightmare, I could still face him at least long enough for the woman to get away.

He turned his attention on me, further warping the surrounding air until it seemed as if we were upside down. That wasn't a problem for me. I spent so much time in shadow that this felt natural.

I charged forward, pulling a blade from shadow essence, much like Robby did with his white one. He jumped back as I slashed for his midsection, but that wasn't my true attack.

Ropes of shadow snaked around the clown, jerking him backward, diving into his chest, his arms, his legs, and draining Nightmare essence from his being, weakening him.

The clown's eyes widened, and juggling knives appeared, floating in the air around us. They gleamed in the twisting light of this warped reality, deadly sharp.

I pulled hard on his energy as he flung them at me.

At the last second, I dissipated completely into black mist. The knives passed through me, relatively harmless, and the clown fled.

I fell to the ground, landing on one knee, as the natural order reasserted itself.

"What the fuck was that?" The woman staggered back to her feet, looking around for her gun. I saw it partially under the bed and tugged it deeper with a tendril of shadow.

"That was a clown. *I* am a Nightmare. You're lucky you're no longer interesting to either of us." I stood just as someone pounded on the door.

"Police! Open up."

I gave her a quick bow and vanished again. She really wasn't having a good day, after all. Part of me hoped she'd talk her way out of her predicament. Part of me didn't have

113

the energy to care. I needed to get back to Ember and the others.

Slipping through the shadows, I really hoped the clown was done with us or that we could get back to Nightmare soon. Though I'd gained some essence from the creature, the entire experience had been more draining than I preferred.

Not only for Dio's sake did we need to get home.

CHAPTER 13

Ember

Robby stepped out of the shadows and thrust a bag at me. I grabbed the black duffle and clutched it to my chest, sensing a strong connection to it. It must have been Dio's essence.

"Nic?"

Robby tightened his lips. "He's facing off against the clown."

"And you left him?" I took a step forward, as if I could go help Nic myself.

"Well, princess, when a prince of Nightmare throws a priceless gem at you and tells you to run, you do."

"Wait, you know how to follow orders?" Ash snarked.

"Ha, ha," Robby replied. He eyed the duffle before turning away. "We will give Nic a minute to return on his own before I go save him."

"We should go rescue Dio tonight," I said. "Once Nic is back. We have to get them back to Nightmare."

"And how, my dear princess, do you propose we do that?" Robby tilted his head as if genuinely curious.

"I really don't know, but the longer Dio and his essence are separated, the more chance the Nightmare creatures have to get one or the other of them. We can't lose Dio." I hugged the black duffle.

Robby nodded. "Obviously."

"You know, sometimes I want to punch you," I muttered.

"It's part of my charm," Robby replied with a grin.

Before we could continue sniping at each other, Nic swirled out of the shadows.

"Nic!" I threw my arms around him. "Are you okay?"

"Yes, Ember. I'm all right."

I saw Nic study Robby before glancing at the duffle I held.

"Should we go tonight?" I clutched the fabric more tightly in my hands.

Nic nodded. "Perhaps Ash can wrangle Casey?" He glanced at my cousin.

"Yeah, sure, shadow boy. What do you want me to tell her?" Ash frowned.

Robby sighed. "I haven't the faintest. Maybe you could lure her back to your place with lyra talk."

Ash chuckled. "I think I'll tell her the truth and see what she makes of it."

The jester's eyes widened. "Perhaps not?"

"Do you think we're safe staying here tonight?" Ash glanced at Nic.

He shrugged. "I truly don't know. I'm not even certain you will be safe at your home."

Ash pursed her lips, then nodded. "I'll get her out of here tonight. I'll think of something. You four be careful."

I hugged Ash. "You're the best, you know that?"

"Don't you forget it." She tightened her arms around me before stepping back. "I need to get my things. You get out of here before you attract those creatures, and I'll take care of Casey. I'll text when we're on our way."

"Thank you, fairest Ash." Robby bowed.

"Who the hell are you, and what have you done with the real Robby?" Ash growled.

The jester chuckled. "You're caring for someone I care about when I cannot. That service requires at least a few flowery words from me."

Ash shook her head and went to the door. "Next time I'm charging. Oh, hey, Nic, remember our discussion about dreams." She left before he could answer.

Robby shot the Nightmare prince a curious look, so Nic explained about Ash's desire to fly in a spaceship.

"Ahh. Perhaps I can manage an appropriate dream for her."

That got me wondering what sorts of dreams I should be looking for from my guys. Of course, the reality of being with Geraint and Nic was better than any dream. Still, maybe...

We quickly gathered our things while I was pondering dreams. Robby went and made his excuses to Casey, and we headed for the van.

***

Still clutching the duffle with Dio's essence, I licked my lips nervously as we drove through the cornfield. Robby had shut the lights off. Enough moonlight filtered down that he could see the road, though he drove slowly. The corn towered on either side of the vehicle, swaying softly in what I hoped was a light breeze and not some supernatural entity. In the dark, the stalks dwarfed the van.

Both not wanting to know if anything peered out at us from the depths of the field, and wanting to know, I alternated between staring straight ahead and glancing into the darkness. My heart clenched, and icy fear tightened my chest and ran through my veins. When we finally broke out of the rows of corn, I wasn't the only one who took a relieved breath.

"Should we have rented a car?" I twisted my hands together. This sneaking around crap was not something I was good at.

"Why?" Nic asked.

Geraint grunted as if just now considering what I'd thought of.

"We're driving a branded vehicle and we're about to sneak into a health care facility and break out someone with a criminal record."

Robby stopped the van and twisted to look at me. "You raise a valid point."

The van shuddered. Robby's eyes went wide, and he slammed on the accelerator. The wheels spun, and the engine whined as if something had a hold of us. Before I could freak out about it, the van lurched forward, fishtailing. Robby got it under control, and we sped down the road for a short distance before the jester slowed again, muttering something that sounded suspiciously like *fucking cornfields*.

"What was that?" I whispered.

"Just the corn," Robby replied in his usual jovial tone. "I will disguise the van, but I suspect the normal concerns of mortal authorities and all that might be less relevant here. This pocket of Dream energy mixing with the conscious realm is, well, very strange, and leads me to believe we are dealing with something other than a normal institution."

"Okay." I hoped he was right. I didn't want my parents to get into trouble.

Robby placed his hand on the dash, and a ripple of energy flowed out from his hand. I didn't see anything different, so I had to trust that he'd disguised us.

We slowed well outside the normal parking area. Robby let the engine idle for a moment while he looked out the windshield. Finally, he shut off the van. We had a fair bit of flat, open ground to cover.

"We'll take a back entrance. Your highness, please shield us with your shadows."

"Of course," Nic said, not acting perturbed that Robby was ordering him around.

We slipped out of the van after Robby deactivated the interior lights and shut the doors gently.

The humidity held the heat of the day and sweat collected between my breasts and under the straps of my bra. Cicadas screamed, drowning out other sounds, which would cover any noise we might make but also prevented us from hearing anything approach. Hopefully, we didn't have to worry about anything sneaking up on us.

Geraint fell back while Robby and Nic took the lead. I tucked myself between the three men and tried to emulate their quiet movements. With Nic's shadows concealing us, we didn't have to worry much about being seen, but it didn't feel right to simply go striding across the grassy lawn as if we owned the place.

Robby led us around to the back of the building and up to a door with a security pad. He put his hand over it, did something, and the door clicked open.

"Well, that's handy," I whispered.

He nodded and slipped inside. We followed. The hallway lights were turned down to a nighttime level, but it felt bright after the moonlight that had lit our way, even with Nic's shadows swirling around us.

Instead of taking the elevator, Robby led us to a stairwell. He worked his magic on the keypads and up we went to the fourth floor. We paused at the door.

Nic held up his hand and slipped into the shadows before we could ask him what was up. He returned a moment later and gestured for us to proceed.

I clutched the bag more tightly against my chest. Though it might have been my imagination, it felt like the energy emanating from the gem thrummed more intensely the closer we got to the Nightmare prince.

We hurried down the hallway, expecting resistance. There had to be someone here doing night checks, didn't there? Or maybe they had a security system that did it for them?

When we made it to Dio's room without trouble, I took a relieved breath. Robby got the door open, and we slipped inside. We stood in the dark, the small nightlight not enough to reveal the room. I wrinkled my nose, not remembering it smelling musky.

Once the door shut behind us, Geraint flipped on the light.

I yelped and jumped behind my knight.

Robby swore, and Nic swirled into shadow while Geraint stepped fully in front of me.

Hundreds of snakes slithered across the floor and up the visible chairs.

"Are they real?" I clutched at my knight's back.

"Real enough," Geraint said as one hissed and struck at him. He backed me into the wall. The snake didn't reach Geraint, but it was close.

Dream energy crackled in the air. Then Robby's legs were sheathed in white armor, like a knight's. He kicked his way through the snakes, sending them flying farther into the room and leaving me and Geraint huddled by the door.

"They were summoned from Nightmare," Nic said, partially solidifying. "Use your shadows to syphon their energy away. Hurry! We have to help Dio."

Trying to get over my revulsion—I didn't hate snakes. I did hate being surrounded by them—I called on my shadow powers. Now that I was more deeply connected to the Dream energy, I could feel what Nic was talking about. I sent out a tendril of shadow to the nearest snake and stabbed it into the creature.

It writhed, trying to fight me. I latched on, taking its energy much like I did when I shared energy with Nic, but there was no return flow in this instance. The snake vanished in a puff of smoke, and I went after another one.

Nic had tendrils in dozens of the snakes, but there were so many.

The bag twitched and jerked out of my hand.

"Hey!" I snatched at it, but I was too late. It hit the ground and rolled into the pile of snakes.

I attacked them with renewed vigor, trying for more than one at a time. I had to get that bag back.

It writhed and my imagination ran wild with the vision of snakes slithering inside the bag, latching onto the gem, and sucking Dio's essence away before we could return it to him.

Tears blurred my vision.

I screamed when the bag burst apart, my heart breaking into shreds as the pieces of the bag vanished into the writhing mass of serpents. Geraint caught my arm as I dove forward, heedless of the danger. He jerked me back as one of the creatures struck, saving me from a nasty bite. I had no idea if nightmare snakes were venomous or not, but I didn't want to find out.

Something burst out of the mass of snakes. Geraint pulled me behind him, shielding me from the creatures as they were flung through the air. A few hit my knight, and he batted them away. *What fresh horror is this?*

A piercing yowl raised the hair on the back of my neck. The sheer rage behind that sound chilled me. I risked a look. An inky black shape spun and twisted, diving at the snakes and tearing them to pieces. Puffs of black smoke obscured a lot of the details, but it looked like some sort of dragon was going to town on the nightmare creatures, tearing them apart.

"What the hell?"

"Princess, some help!" Robby snapped.

"Sorry, sorry." I went back to attacking the snakes, gaining confidence and energy as I went. With the dragon's help, we managed to destroy the nightmare.

I made it the rest of the way into the room in time to see Robby yank one last serpent off of a prone Dio and fling it away. The creature that had burst out of the duffle bag pounced on it and tore it apart. I suspected it had absorbed a lot of the energy from the nightmare like I had. I felt full, nearly to bursting.

The creature hopped up on the bed, black coat glistening, wings outstretched, feline tail swishing back and forth idly. I took a closer look. That wasn't a dragon. That was a small, winged panther or a very large, winged house cat. My fingers itched to stroke that soft fur. Even the creature's wings were covered in fur and if it weren't for the murder mittens it currently flexed on Dio's bed, the thing would have looked like a large, cuddly stuffed animal.

I glanced at Nic. He studied the creature, brow furrowed in concentration. Robby cast about the room, probably looking for other nightmares.

"What is that?" I gasped.

Nic turned his attention to me. "Dio's essence."

I raised my eyebrows. "It looks like a flying cat?"

A mysterious smile ghosted across Nic's lips before he nodded. "Yes, apparently it does."

The creature hopped up onto Dio's stomach and purred, kneading his chest without unsheathing its claws. The creature looked shiny and healthy. Dio, on the other hand, looked awful. His curls were limp and plastered in sweat, his dusky skin ashen, and he looked thin as if he'd lost weight in the few days since we'd last seen him.

"What do we do?" I came over to Dio's side and put my hand on his arm. I didn't dare pet the winged cat, much as I wanted to. Dio's skin felt cool and clammy to my touch. I blinked away tears.

"I don't know," Nic said. "I had thought simply bringing his essence to him would be enough. That I know of, no one has ever done what he did before."

My phone vibrated in my pocket, startling me. I pulled it out and stared at the screen. Ash wouldn't be calling me if it wasn't important. She knew what we were up to. Dread tightened its icy grip on me, squeezing my chest as I hit reply.

"Ash?"

"Ember, they said you have to come and bring the beast with you, or they'll kill us." Ash's tight voice conveyed the depth of her anger and a hint of her fear.

"Where are you?"

"My place."

"We're about an hour away."

"I know. Be careful."

"You, too."

I hung up and turned my attention to the guys. Robby's eyes tightened, and he clenched his fists at his side. "I'm going to spy on them," he said, handing me the keys to the van before he vanished.

"Nic?"

"Obviously, Robby expects us to follow. We should get Dio out of here. We may not be able to fix him until we're back in Nightmare. We'll just have to defeat the clown and whoever is with him, then figure out how to get home."

"Right, simple."

Nic smiled. "I never said any of this would be easy, luv."

I forced a smile. "I know."

"Knight, could you collect Dio?"

Geraint nodded. "As long as the cat lets me."

As if understanding Geraint's words, the creature backed off, sitting and licking his paw, wings tucked along its back.

Geraint heaved Dio over his shoulder in a rescue carry. The winged panther hopped off the bed and padded along behind us, wings tucked tightly to his back. Nic wrapped us in shadows, and we slipped out into the hallway.

Though nerve-wracking, the trip back to the van went quickly. I got behind the wheel, adjusting the seat forward so I could reach the petals, then firing up the engine. Trying to hurry while being quiet and discrete, I hit the driveway and attempted to ignore the cornfields that loomed in the distance.

Robby popped back in, making me scream and jerk the wheel.

"Easy, princess."

"Damn it, Robby," I snarled.

"There are two clowns." He sounded uncharacteristically grim.

"Amazing," I muttered sarcastically.

Nic melted into shadow for a moment. "We must draw them into Dream."

"When you figure out how we're going to do that, let me know." Robby's tension manifested in his uncharacteristically sharp tone.

"Go watch them, jester. We'll come up with a plan," Nic ordered.

Robby vanished again.

124

"Ember. It is possible you can create a pathway for us. As Robby has pointed out, the entire point of having a mortal in our grouping is to add the energy of creation to Dream and keep the energies fresh."

I'd been having thoughts along those lines and nodded. "Okay."

"That may be our only recourse," Nic continued.

"No pressure or anything." I clenched my hands on the wheel.

"We'll likely die if you don't figure it out." Nic gripped my shoulder.

"Lovely." I turned and glared at Nic.

"So, you know, we're all going to die?" Geraint interjected.

"Hey!"

He smiled at me from the passenger seat. "I have complete faith in you, Spark."

That really didn't make me feel better, but I focused on my driving instead, breathing a sigh of relief when we broke free of the cornfields. I flipped on the lights and hit the accelerator, driving as quickly as I dared toward Ash's place.

***

A small eternity later, I pulled up in front of Ash's house.

"What do we do?" I hated how small my voice sounded.

"Front door, probably," Geraint replied grimly.

"I agree. They know we're coming." Nic dissolved mostly into shadow before exiting the van. He solidified once he stood on the sidewalk.

I stared out into the night. Clouds obscured the moon and the stars, not to mention light pollution from the city.

125

I'd lost track of the time and when I glanced at the clock, it was nearly two in the morning. No wonder I was exhausted.

We got out of the truck. Geraint hefted Dio over his shoulders again, and we headed for the front door. I dragged my feet, and I pressed my hands against my stomach, trying to suppress the butterflies that churned my guts.

As soon as we stepped onto the small front porch, the air around us rippled and warped. After having dealt with the snakes, it was easier to feel the Dream energy that the clowns used to do their magic, or whatever you wanted to call it.

"Can we—?"

Nic held up his hand, interrupting me. He tapped his ear, and I took that to mean we could be overheard so I fell silent. That left me wondering if we could absorb the clowns' energy like we had with the snakes, though.

The door opened at my touch, swinging inward without me having to turn the knob. We entered, worry for Ash and Casey hurrying our steps. Fear churned my stomach.

Ash had a large mirror in her entryway. I didn't want to look, but movement drew my eye. Two clowns stared at me, one somewhat taller than the other. I recognized the taller one from before. The shorter clown had a rounder face and slightly more feminine features under the white face paint.

They both smiled, showing pointed teeth. The taller one gestured toward the living room.

The cat hissed, but we all did what they ordered. Tremors wracked my body and my legs felt like jelly, making it hard to comply with the clowns.

I knew from many past visits that mirrors lined one wall in her living room, and she had her lyra hung in front

126

of them. The other half of the room contained the normal couch, loveseat, gas fireplace, and coffee table.

Nothing had changed, except Robby sprawled unconscious on the ground in front of the coffee table, and Casey and Ash were bound and gagged on the couch. Ash looked pissed as hell. Terror had widened Casey's red-puffy eyes, and tears streaked her face.

The two clowns, the man wearing the gray suit, and a shorter, plumper woman also wearing a gray suit stood in front of the fireplace, amused smirks on their faces. The mirror reflected their true natures, and I tried to avoid looking at it while I thought furiously about how I was going to get us out of this.

Maybe if I opened an arch in the mirror, I could drag their reflections through? Of course, first I had to open an arch.

Since I wanted to use the mirror, I moved to place myself in front of it. The lyra spun gently when I bumped it with my shoulder. Wincing, I rubbed the spot.

Geraint stood next to me with Dio still slung over his shoulder, and Nic kneeled by Robby, not bothering to hide his shadowy nature. Casey's eyes widened further. The cat stalked into the room like it owned the place, tail lashing.

The female clown darted forward, trying to catch it. It turned on her, hissing and unsheathing some truly impressive claws. Turns out, clowns bleed red just like humans do. She shrieked in anger, and the air wavered around us.

"You will leave that with us." The male clown pointed at Dio. "Then you can leave."

Nic rose to his feet, the shadows swirling furiously around his feet. "I am a prince of Nightmare. You do not give me commands. You will return with us to Nightmare, and you will be dealt with."

The clowns laughed.

Nic glanced at me, then at the mirror, before returning his attention to the creatures. The ground rippled as the clowns called on their powers. I let him deal with the clowns for now, while I turned my attention to getting us back to Nightmare.

Casey squealed through her gag, and the ground shifted under my feet. I kept my back to whatever was going on, trusting Nic to defend us to the best of his abilities. Ash also yelled angrily, and I suspected it had more to do with the potential damage to her house than anything.

I pressed my hand to the mirror and touched it with the shadow essence I held, folding it into a sort of gateway with my mind and picturing the cabin in the woods we'd used to get back and forth many times.

A clown appeared in front of me. The woman. Blood dripped from her lips as she bared her sharp teeth and brandished a juggling dagger.

Screaming, I jerked back.

She lunged forward.

I wasn't fast enough, and hot fire stabbed into my gut. Flailing, I grabbed Ash's lyra, trying to stop my fall to the ground. All the energy I'd been about to throw at the mirror left me, and pain filled my awareness. Distantly, I heard someone yell my name. Hands gripped me, but I couldn't think beyond the agony spreading through my body.

CHAPTER 14

Geraint

I'd thought I'd known what being powerless felt like before, when we'd first been taken to Nightmare. That feeling paled compared to the gut-wrenching agony of watching Ember fall to the ground, a blossom of red spreading from her abdomen.

"Nic!" I yelled as I dumped Prince Dio to the ground and clutched Ember to me.

The cat creature screamed in rage and savaged the clown that had injured my spark.

"We have to get back to Dream!" Nic shouted.

"Why?" I snarled. Even I could tell the injury was fatal.

"Because in people's dreams, healing potions exist," Nic replied. "I don't think sharing essence with her will save her from such a wound."

That was all well and good, but we still had no idea how to get back to the Dream realm.

Ash slammed into my shoulder with her hip. I looked up, eyes going wide. Her lyra spun gently, and inside the hoop of metal the air shone like a mirror. Ember had done it.

"Nic!"

The shadow prince threw a shadowy net at the clowns before twisting around, glaring at me. I pointed up. His eyebrows rose, and he nodded. "Go!"

The clowns seemed to realize they were going to lose their prize. Reality returned to normal, settling around us. Then one of them threw a round object at the fireplace. Gas flared, sparked, and caught fire.

The flames spread.

"Fuck!" Ash yelled through her gag. Her hands were still bound behind her. Casey had managed to get her hands in front of her, and she pulled on Robby's limp arm.

"Go help Casey," I shouted.

Ash turned, and I took one hand from Ember's stomach and helped her get the ropes off. She yanked the gag from her mouth as she ran to Casey's side.

Nic grabbed Dio and tossed him through the arch. We had no idea where it went, but at this point, we were out of options. Ash and Casey dragged Robby over. Nic grabbed him with his shadows and tossed him through the lyra-arch, too. The winged cat followed.

"You two must get out of here," Nic pointed frantically toward the lyra.

The gas line exploded.

Nic shielded us from the worst of the blast with his shadows, but the house would be consumed.

Casey dove through the lyra before we could stop her. Before Ash could head for a window and freedom, the walls shimmered, warping into solid mirrors like a demented, burning *fun* house.

"Fuck!" Ash screamed again in rage before diving through the arch.

Nic helped me get Ember off the ground. "Go, Knight. It will probably close once she's through it. I can fit with her."

Letting Nic take my spark, I went through the arch, knowing he'd be right behind me.

We spilled out of the lyra into a very familiar-looking cabin. At first, I thought that perhaps we'd simply gone back to the woods outside our childhood home, then the chill energy of Nightmare settled into my skin, and I knew we'd returned to the place I'd been created.

Ash and Casey were screwed, but they were alive.

Nic stepped through and, as he'd said, the arch snapped shut behind him. He set Ember on the table and vanished, returning moments later with a clear glass bottle full of bright red liquid.

He tipped Ember's head back and poured some of the liquid into her mouth.

For a moment, nothing happened. Then she took a gasping breath and rolled over onto her side, coughing. Nic and I held her while she recovered from the nearly fatal stab.

"Where are we?" Casey breathed past a sob.

Ember's eyes widened, and she sat upright. "You weren't supposed to come." She looked back and forth between Casey and Ash. "No! Oh no—."

"Ember, we didn't have a choice. It was this or burning up in the fire," Ash had her lawyer face on, but her eyes glistened with unshed tears.

"But..." Ember pressed her bloody hand to her face, then jerked it away. "Ew. Wait, why am I not dead?"

Nic held up the empty bottle. "Healing cordial."

"Why didn't we give one of those to Geraint when he was hurt?" Ember's eyes narrowed.

"As much as this did not take me long to procure, they are rare. Those of us in possession of one are wise to save them for truly life-threatening injuries. I'll have to find another." He set the bottle down. "Also, at the time, I would not have wasted it on a knight."

131

Ember's lips tightened. "And now?"

"I would save him as long as it didn't mean losing you."

I put my hand on Ember's shoulder. "That's fair," I said before she could reply. "I wouldn't want you to choose me over her. Ever."

"Robby?" Casey shoved at his shoulder, interrupting us.

Nic sighed and kneeled by the jester. "He'll be all right. Knight, please stand guard."

Though I wasn't exactly happy at getting ordered around, it certainly wasn't the time to argue. Likely it never would be. He was one of the rulers of Nightmare, after all.

I went outside, took a quick look around, and rushed back in. "We have to leave. Now."

"What's wrong?" Ember demanded.

"Nothingness storm."

Nic swore and slammed his palm down on Robby's chest. His hand swirled into shadow and melded with the jester.

Robby came awake like he'd been shocked, jerking up off the ground and swinging at Nic, who simply dissolved completely. Robby's fist passed through Nic's shadow.

The jester blinked a few times, looked around, then swore when he saw where we were while taking in Ash and Casey staring at him. "That was not supposed to happen."

"We'll explain later," Nic said. "Nothingness storm." Nic grabbed Dio with his shadows. The winged cat stayed close.

Robby scrambled to his feet, and I led the way out of the crowded one-room cabin. He put his arm around Casey to comfort her as she made a distressed sound at the stark Nightmare landscape.

"It's going to destroy the cabin," Ember cried, pointing.

The storm bore down on us. We were too close to run.

"Shadow boy, remember that spaceship I asked for?" Ash pointed toward the sky.

Nic widened his eyes before holding his hands above his head, sending out tendrils of his power until he acted like he grabbed something and yanked back. Moments later, a spinning saucer appeared above us.

"Next time I'll get one from Dream, but this was closer," Nic said tightly.

A beam of light grabbed all of us and pulled us up into the saucer, very much like a B-Movie abduction. Which I supposed this could be a nightmare of.

Before I knew it, we were all onboard. A bunch of little green men in silver jumpsuits holding ray guns and things that looked suspiciously like probes stared at us.

Nic shoved them back with his powers, and Robby dashed for a room off to the side.

"Wait, you can fly a spaceship?" Ash's eyes widened and shock made her voice crack.

"Sure, why not?" Robby couldn't fit into the pilot's chair, but he grabbed the controls and caused us to speed away from the blight that threatened to wipe us out of existence.

Ash joined him, staring out the front window.

"So, why didn't we use a spaceship to travel before?" Ember asked. "Not that I minded the wolves, or walking, or the horses, but this is much faster."

"Truthfully, I didn't think of it," Nic answered.

"Nor did I." Robby shook his head. "I was never much of a sci-fi fan. It simply didn't occur to me to take a ship."

"When is someone going to explain what is going on?" Casey held up her hands when one of the green men pointed its laser at her.

"Take us to your leader," it demanded.

We all pointed to Nic.

He thrust his hands toward the beings and tendrils of shadow touched each of the aliens. They went still, as if no longer animated.

"We will explain," Robby said. "Once we're safe. We need a place to regroup."

Ember sagged, and I put my arm around her waist. "Yeah, maybe a nap?" she said.

"It has been a trying day," Nic agreed.

I snorted. "Understatement."

Ash ran a hand through her hair and shot me a bleak look.

"Oh, Ash," Ember said, voice cracking with her sorrow.

Her cousin turned away, waving her hand in dismissal. "It's fine."

Ember shut her eyes and took a deep breath. We'd certainly have to deal with all this later, but for now I held my spark while Robby steered us away from the Nothingness storm.

The winged cat trilled, and we turned to look at him. It pawed at Dio. The fallen prince didn't respond. I wasn't even sure he was breathing.

Nic went to his brother's side and put his hand on Dio's shoulder. The other he put on the cat.

"Ember, come here, if you will, and see if you can syphon the cat's energy back into Dio."

She pulled away from me and sat next to the unconscious prince. When she held out her hand to the cat, it rubbed against her, purring. My spark put her other hand on Dio's chest, and she shut her eyes.

The cat didn't object as she pulled on his energy and funneled it back into the Nightmare prince. The cat faded, not unlike when Nic joined with his shadows, until nothing remained of the winged feline.

Dio's chest rose and fell a few times before he snapped his eyes open. He stared at Nic before his gaze darted to Ember.

"Princess," he breathed out, his light Middle Eastern accent making the title sound exotic.

"Dio!" She gasped, hand going to her mouth.

He struggled to sit. Nic tried to restrain him, but he batted his brother's hand away, so Nic helped him sit instead.

"I thought you were a dream," he said.

"A really good one, I hope," she joked, though I sensed uncertainty in her. She glanced at me before allowing Dio to pull her into a hug.

He buried his face against her neck and crushed her to his chest. "You smell just like I remember," he said.

I shifted, wondering how he would react when he caught my scent all over her. If his essence took on the shape of a cat, I bet he had a better than average sense of smell. Hopefully, we could avoid that confrontation until we'd dealt with some of the other problems facing us. Like Ash and Casey and how we were going to explain to the lyrist that she was trapped in the Dream realm for the rest of her life. Ash already knew, though I doubted she'd really comprehended what that meant.

Dio glanced at his brother before he turned his attention to me, eyes narrowing.

So clearly we were going to deal with this now. Shit.

CHAPTER 15

Ember

Dio's attention shifted from me and Nic to Geraint. He couldn't possibly have already figured out Geraint and I were involved, could he?

The low growl that thrummed through his chest made me think that somehow he had.

I scrambled to my feet and put myself between the two men, backing until I leaned against Geraint's chest. There wasn't a lot of room on the spaceship, so it didn't put a ton of space between me and Dio, but it was enough.

"You are my princess, not his," Dio growled. "He will die for touching you."

"I'm not your anything," I bit out. "And if you want me to be your princess, you'll have to accept Geraint."

"Dio," Nic said. "Not now."

Dio swung around, glaring at Nic.

"We have bigger problems to deal with."

"She is ours, brother."

Nic shrugged. "She's mine, she's the knight's, and if you can get your head out of your ass, she might well be yours, but it's her choice."

Dio growled, and I could practically envision the winged feline standing next to him, lashing his tail.

I glared right back at him. "The world is literally being erased around us. Nightmare is falling to ruin, two of my friends just became dreambound, and a whole shit ton

137

of other bad things are happening. We still have to find the real Baz, and I can't even think of what else right now. Maybe, just maybe, leave off the possessive BS until later. Okay?"

Dio spun away and stalked to the far end of the open space in the middle of the saucer. I glanced at Nic, who shook his head and swirled into shadow for a moment.

Geraint took my hand, and I tugged him into the cockpit with Casey, Robby, and Ash. It was crowded with all of us in there, but Geraint wrapped his arms around me, and we tucked into a corner, trying not to touch any of the mysterious buttons or flashing green lights.

"Well, it sure is pretty," Ash said, voice neutral.

The view port showed a vibrant landscape full of verdant valleys, rocky mountains, literal rainbow-filled waterfalls, herds of animals running across grassy plains, sweeping rivers, and other beautiful landscapes all contained under a brilliant blue sky with puffy clouds.

I hoped the clouds in Dream weren't as carnivorous as the ones in Nightmare. Otherwise, they might come after the saucer.

Robby brought us down in a large grassy field. "The saucer is going to want to return to the darker side of Dream as soon as I let go of the controls. Go ahead, get off here," he said. "I'll meet you outside."

We coaxed Casey from Robby's side. Nic had already figured out how to lower the ramp, and he and Dio waited at the base of the saucer. We hurried out. The ramp closed behind us, and the saucer lifted off.

"He's leaving us?" Casey yelped.

"No, dearest. I'm not."

She yelped again as Robby appeared from nothing, as he often did.

"I don't understand. What is going on?" Tears streamed from Casey's eyes, and Robby folded her against his side.

"We'll explain shortly. While we should be safer in Dream than in Nightmare, I'd rather get indoors." Robby pointed toward a path that wound into the deep woods.

Nic, dragging Dio by the arm, went down the path Robby indicated. Geraint hung back to watch behind us, and I stayed close to my knight.

"Well, that went well," Geraint muttered.

"I didn't have to tackle him," I pointed out.

"I rather hope it doesn't come to that, my spark." He caressed my pet name with his voice, making me glow inside.

"I feel like I'm in a Disney movie." The birdsong sounded a little too perfect. The grass and underbrush were too evenly spaced, and the trees were a bit too uniform. I wasn't going to complain about the comfortable temperature, however.

"If we were in that sort of movie," Geraint replied. "We'd have to worry about a monster to defeat around the bend."

"Ahh, point. But, I suppose, in a way, we do have to worry about that."

Geraint gave me a tight smile. "I think I need to find a weapon. Robby and Prince Nic have magic. I just have me."

"You're magic enough on your own, Knight." I kissed him to make sure he knew I wasn't really joking.

Geraint chuckled. "What would I do without you, Spark?"

"I'm rather hoping you don't have to find out."

On those grim words, we fell silent. The soft thud and crunch of our feet on the dirt path, and the sound of our breathing blended into the perfect symphony of birds and insects and rustling leaves that made up the background noise.

It didn't take long for us to reach the cabin at the end of the path. I turned and looked back, but the trail we'd taken blended into the forest so well I wasn't sure I'd be able to find it again.

Goosebumps prickled my arms, and an icy chill trailed down my back when I inspected the cabin Robby had brought us to.

"I thought you said we'd be safe here." I glared at the jester.

"Yes, Princess. While candy-coated cabins in the forest are not typically as safe as they might otherwise appear, as long as we don't actually eat any of the candy, we'll be perfectly safe. These are transitional places. They start in Dream, but sometimes end up in Nightmare. This particular cabin originated with the fairy tales, but it also does double duty as a childhood fancy for kids who have played certain video games that are much kinder to hungry children in the woods. We will be safe."

"As long as we don't eat the candy?" My stomach disagreed with that plan. The delicious, sugary smell had filtered over to me, and it had exerted its own siren call on my sweet tooth.

Nic smiled and swirled into mist, disappearing for a few moments. Dio's expression darkened to an annoyed glare.

When Nic returned he placed a hand on the cabin, pulled off a gingerbread wafer, and popped it in its mouth. We all waited, but when nothing happened, he relaxed. "I closed the connection to Nightmare. It will reopen eventually, but we don't have to worry right now."

Casey laughed bitterly. "Right. No one is worried about anything. Sure... Just eat the house. Like that's normal?"

My momentary relief disappeared. "Right. So, I guess we've got a lot to tell you."

Robby tightened his lips and put his arm around Casey. "Let's go inside and we'll fill you in."

***

I stared around the cabin while Robby told Casey everything. We'd left him to explain things to her since it was essentially his fault she was involved. I listened, but he stuck to topics I was already familiar with. Ash stood with her hands behind her back, staring into the fireplace. A small fire crackled merrily, and a fortunately empty—I'd checked—stew pot hung nearby.

Hunger had gotten the better of me, and I wandered about nibbling on the house while I explored. Now I sat on the marshmallow cushioned couch and marveled at the way people's dreams had shaped this particular cabin.

Like many dream structures, the interior design didn't quite make sense, and a few doors that looked like they should lead outside led to other rooms, but it was cozy enough without the danger of ending up in a nightmare. It also repaired itself after you took a bite of it. Handy, that.

Casey's look of horror and Ash's tight shoulders told me all I needed to know about how they felt about their new circumstances.

"I'm trapped here?" Casey cried out when Robby got to the part about them being dreambound. "I can't leave?"

"No, dear. At least we've not yet discovered a way to send mortals home once they reach Dream."

"But..." She turned her attention to me. "Ember goes back and forth?"

"Ember is Nightmare's princess," Robby replied gently. "The same rules do not apply to her."

"So I'm trapped in a land that is slowly getting erased, and if we don't fix it we're all going to die anyway?" She curled into Robby's arms and wiped at her cheeks.

"Yes."

"Just great," she muttered.

I went over to the nearest gingerbread wall and snapped a piece off, more to have something to do with my hands than still being hungry.

"Casey, we will speak to the king and queen once we've saved Dream," Robby assured her.

"All we have to do is find this Baz guy, hope those four can work things out, wish them a good love life and everything will be okay?" Casey's voice cracked on every other word, but she did seem to grasp our situation.

"There may be more to it than that," Nic said. "But finding Baz is the next step."

"'K. How do we do that?" Casey straightened a little, though Robby kept his arm around her.

"First, we get some rest," Nic said.

A yawn stopped my protest. I didn't want to rest. I wanted to get this resolved so we could start figuring out how to help Ash and Casey.

Geraint took my hand and tugged me toward the back of the cabin where some of the bedrooms had been.

I stopped by Ash, putting my hand on her back.

"I'm all right, Ember. I'd rather be stuck here than dead. It's just a lot to process right now. Get some sleep. I want to try out that marshmallow couch." She turned and smiled sadly at me.

I nodded and resumed my quest for a bed. Nic could join us if he wanted.

Dio stepped into my path, glaring at Geraint.

"What do you think you're doing, knight?"

I sighed. "You do remember the part where who I share a bed with isn't any of your business, right?"

Dio stepped forward until his chest was in my face. He was taller, like Nic. My heart raced in fear, but I refused to back down, knowing he wouldn't hurt me.

"You are my princess," he growled. "It is my business, and you are not sleeping with a knight. He will die for his trespass."

"Wow, old-fashioned ideals and jealous, controlling assholes are so sexy," Ash said sarcastically. "And people wonder why I don't date men."

Dio frowned, distracted by Ash's biting comments. "What?"

"You heard me, asshole. Now go find your own place to sleep and leave Ember and Geraint alone." Ash came up behind me.

Nic swirled into being next to Dio.

"Yeah, you're not very attractive when you're being a dick," Casey added from the couch where she still sat with Robby.

"I think I liked you better when you didn't have your essence," I finished. "You weren't like this when we were kids or I'm not sure I would have enjoyed your company then. I'm certainly not enjoying it now. Move." I jabbed him in the chest and for a wonder, he backed off.

Though I kept myself between him and my knight, he didn't try anything when I pulled Geraint past. I picked the first door I came to and pulled Knight inside with me.

"Spark," Geraint said hesitantly. "This is a closet."

"Fuck," I muttered.

He chuckled. "At least it's a linen closet. We'll make it work. Come on. Let's get some rest."

"Biggest linen closet I've ever seen." It was basically a walk in full of blankets and sheets. We pulled a bunch

143

down and made ourselves a nest. Geraint curled around me and, feeling safe, I drifted off.

Before I'd fully fallen asleep, Geraint whispered in my ear. "It's super sexy when you defend me like that."

I curled my lips in a smile. "You usually take care of me. Nice to be able to return the favor."

***

Morning brought a sugary breakfast, a few surly glances from Dio, and a brilliant sunrise that we somehow got to see when we went outside for a few minutes, though I swore we had slept in hours past when the sun should have been high in the sky.

Nic had joined us for a while last night, but he'd spent most of the time keeping watch while the rest of us rested.

Dio looked tired today, sitting slumped in one of the marshmallow chairs. I suspected yesterday his essence had been energized by feeding on all that energy from the snakes. Today, he was likely feeling the effects of the long separation between his body and his essence.

I wasn't ready to deal with his attitude, though I was glad he was back in one piece. Casey looked like she hadn't slept, but Ash seemed like herself today.

"All right, shadow boy, if I'm going to be stuck here, I want a stabby unicorn. How do I get one?" Ash clunked her mug down on the table for emphasis.

Nic studied her gravely. "We will work on it. Let's see if we can find Baz first."

"Fine, but then we're going unicorn hunting," Ash insisted.

Nic inclined his head in agreement while Dio glowered at all of us.

Casey glanced up hopefully at Robby.

"We'll see, dearest," he replied, rubbing soothing circles on her back.

At least he seemed to be taking his responsibilities to Casey seriously. I shook my head. Having known Robby for years, I never would have thought he'd take to Casey the way he had. He'd always gone for the one-night stands or very short hookups. I supposed being a Dream jester explained a lot of that. Maybe they'd be able to stay together. My gaze shifted to Dio. I wondered if he'd always been this possessive or if it was a newer thing. He had always shared everything with his brothers and me, and I'd never seen him interact with anyone outside of our small group, so it was possible this was simply how he was.

"We should head out. I'm going to walk around. Find me when you're all ready." I pushed my chair back and stood, deliberately running my hand across Geraint's shoulders before going over and giving Nic a quick kiss. Then I went outside, enjoying the cool breeze as it caressed my cheeks. It carried an intoxicating scent I couldn't help but follow.

It led me to a patch of wildflowers of every imaginable color. Delighted with the variety, I kneeled, wishing I had my sketch pad with me. When things settled down, I was going to travel Dream and draw everything I could.

Leaning forward, I inhaled deeply, pulling the intoxicating scent deep into my lungs.

CHAPTER 16

Dio

Memories

"**P**rinces, why do I sense a connection between you and the conscious realm?" Our instructor, Plato, was from the dream side of Dream realm. He traveled back and forth and taught us and the Dream princesses. We met with the princesses a few times a year and saw the king and queen then, as well. They were technically our parents, but we weren't born the same way humans were.

We all shared a confused look. We knew going to the conscious realm couldn't form any sort of connection. Yeah, we had a friend there, but Ember was just a friend. We'd been playing with her for years.

"We don't know what you're talking about, Professor," Baz said for all of us.

Plato's frown deepened. He tucked his hands into the robes he wore and paced in front of us, thinking. The gray gravel that made up the ground crunched under his feet, and the cool breeze swirled his long robes.

I knew that expression and he wouldn't address us again until he was good and ready. Plato told us he'd been formed based on a Greek philosopher, and he took his origins seriously, which is how he'd ended up as our teacher.

"You three will come with me. We're going to the palace."

We all shared another concerned look. That wasn't good. Usually, we enjoyed going to Dream Palace, but Plato was upset and that didn't bode well for us. What connection could he possibly be talking about?

Not having a choice in the matter, we all stood and followed Plato into Nightmare castle. He preferred to instruct us outside.

We stopped in front of the big mirror in the ballroom. All castles and palaces had to have a ballroom, or so Plato claimed. I couldn't see why. We never used it except to travel. Shouldn't it be called the traveling room? Well, I supposed we used it once a year. Human dreams filled it with pumpkins and bats and ghouls and skeletons. The vampires and other monsters usually made an appearance, too.

"Lady." Plato bowed to the mirror and a ghostly woman in white flowing robes appeared. There were a lot of mirror people that helped dream creatures travel, but those from Dream typically asked The Lady in White for assistance, while we used Bloody Mary.

"Hello, Professor," she said, her voice wispy and sad.

"Lady, could you please take us to Dream Palace?"

"Of course." She backed away from the mirror and a lane of flowering trees with pink blooms and arching branches that touched, making a tunnel, shimmered in the mirror before us.

Plato gestured for us to go through. We all thanked the Lady as we pushed into the cool surface of the mirror and stepped into its depths. The path she created let us out into Dream Palace's ballroom. A couple of dreams waltzed to music only they and their dreamer could hear. One pair vanished as their imaginer lost the threads of the dream. The other pair remained quite solid, though their waltz faltered, and the man bent to kiss the woman. They wouldn't remain in the ballroom long.

I averted my gaze and followed Plato and my brothers. The nightmares about sex weren't nearly as pleasant as the dreams were, and I'd never grown fond of watching them. Even though I knew this one would likely go the way the imaginer wanted, I didn't want to watch in case it shifted. Dreams were fickle things.

We made our way through the opal hallways and crystalline corridors toward the throne room, where the king and queen would be waiting. I didn't think they spent all their time there, but that's always where we found them.

The guards opened the big double doors for us, and we entered the opulent hall. I preferred the blacks and grays and muted colors of Nightmare Castle, but the hall was impressive and beautiful. Humanity's dreams had blended to mix fantasy with their reality and form Dream Palace. From what I knew of the conscious realm, the styles came from the best of each type of architecture and mixed with fantasy elements like what they thought elves might live in.

Plato bowed to the Queen of Loss and the King of Hope. The queen was tall, slender, and wore long black robes, and shrouded her face with a lacy black veil, very much in contrast to the king and her surroundings. The king wore purple and gold, and nearly always greeted us with an enormous smile. We were products of the dream energy that had been used to create us, after all.

"My royal highnesses," Plato said. "I'm sensing a connection between the Nightmare princes and the conscious realm. Do you know what this is about?"

The queen stepped down from her throne and approached us. "We do not," she replied before placing her hand on Baz's forehead.

149

"It appears they have created a bond with a human. This is their mate bond." She raised her eyebrows and studied the three of us.

It probably helped our cause that we all felt as confused as Plato was when she said those words. What human? How? The only human we interacted with was Ember.

"What do you mean?" Nic finally asked.

"You have chosen your human mate. Who are they?"

We all looked at each other, then back at the Queen. "Don't you have to, like, have a ceremony and stuff?" I asked. At those words, a memory tugged at me, and a cold thrill ran through my veins. A couple of years ago, we had played at a wedding with Ember, but that was just a game, and if that had caused this, why were they only noticing it now?

"Yes, Dio, you do have to have a ceremony. Who is the human?"

I met Nic's gaze. His expression hardened, eyes narrowing, and he swirled into shadow, hands clenched at his side. Baz still looked confused, but the chill I felt lightened to warmth. *We got to keep her? Forever?* Best day ever!

CHAPTER 17

Dio

I ached to touch Ember. It was as if I were incomplete, and nothing but her presence would fix me. It wasn't even a sexual desire. I needed to feel her skin against mine. But I'd screwed everything up.

Nic had taken the time to explain why she was with her knight, not that it made me feel any better. He'd also told me he'd absolutely destroy me if I did anything to hurt her, and I believed him. At one point we would have been equal in a fight of that sort, and I might have risked it, but I'd been incapacitated for years, and weakness tugged at my limbs and pulled at my eyelids. I wanted to sleep for a year to recover from what I'd done to myself. It had been necessary, but I was paying for it now.

When Ember left the cabin, I almost followed to see if I could apologize to her. I'd never stop feeling possessive, but maybe I could be less of an asshole about it. My exhaustion warred with my need to stalk prey through the darkness, stretch my legs and run, or take to the skies. I wanted to move, but I could barely lift my hand to feed myself.

After a bit, I glanced at the door again. She'd said we needed to get going, and I was sure she was right. Why was everyone else sitting here staring at me?

"Dio, go after her," Nic finally ordered.

I clenched my hands into fists and glared at my brother. "She does not want me to."

"You're so certain?" Nic crossed his arms over his chest then faded partially into shadow, as he often did.

"Fairly." Admittedly, I could barely think through my exhaustion.

"We don't have time for you two to avoid each other. Go talk to her." Nic solidified and pointed at the door.

Reluctantly, I stood.

"While you are attempting to grovel, I will procure transportation for us." The jester left the cabin, the mortal he'd dragged through to Dream clinging to him. I still wasn't clear on why we were traveling with a court jester. They were obnoxious at best. I still wasn't clear on a lot of things. Nic had only taken the time to warn me about what would happen if I continued to threaten the knight.

I supposed there would be time enough for questions later. I avoided looking at the knight as I left the cabin, though I could feel his attention on me. He'd kept her safe and kept her from falling for a random mortal while we were unable to reach her. I should be grateful for that. But did he have to claim her as his own?

The growl that leaked from my lips let me know I had a long way to go before I could accept the knight, but if I couldn't kill him, I'd have to work on it. I still wasn't convinced I would let him live, but for now, we had to focus on finding Baz.

I sniffed the air, finding Ember's trail. I always associated her spring breeze scent with the conscious realm and my childhood, but it was uniquely her scent and my beast wanted to roll around in it. I wanted to roll around in it. Giving in to some of my baser instincts, I slipped into the forest, quieting my footsteps, and stalking her through the woods. There was never a time when I was happier than when stalking prey through challenging terrain, unless I was stalking Ember.

This trail wasn't a challenge, which, today, was okay. Maybe soon we could play in the labyrinth, or in borderland forests. The thought of chasing her delicious spring breeze scent through the wilds of Nightmare gave me a burst of energy, and the weight in my limbs lightened for a few steps.

Another scent crowded over the top of Ember's. The pungent aroma of fantasy blossoms curled through the air. They fed off mortal dream energy and were relatively harmless for the sleepers, trading intense dreams for their sustenance. They were the reason mortals woke tired from particularly vivid dreams. The flowers were not harmless to creatures of the realm who might happen upon them and get snared in their trap. They would sap the dream being's energy until the creature had none left to give and vanished, as they were unable to wake and escape the blooms. Essentially dying until a dreamer re-birthed it in some other incarnation. A mortal caught in their heady fragrance would likely die.

I hastened, giving up the chase in favor of speed, in case Ember was ensnared.

Pausing at the edge of the patch of blossoms, I saw my fears had been justified. Ember kneeled, surrounded by vibrant blooms, eyes shut, an expression of peaceful bliss on her face. Though it seemed cruel to wake her from whatever pleasant dream held her, leaving her would be far worse.

I stomped through the flowers, crushing blossoms and stems, angry at them for endangering my princess.

"Ember," I snarled.

When she didn't reply, I lunged forward and grabbed her around the waist. She went limp when I stood her up, so I threw her over my shoulders and staggered out of the patch before the fragrance could pull me under. Already it tugged at my exhaustion, promising sleep in the arms of my princess. If I hadn't known better, I would have succumbed.

I rushed out of the deadly patch of flowers toward fresher air, staggering under Ember's weight. She wasn't overly heavy, but my limbs had little extra strength. I made it back to the clearing around the sugary cabin and gently lowered her to the ground, collapsing next to her, gasping for breath.

"What happened?" That damn knight came out, followed by Nic and Ember's cousin.

"Fantasy blossoms." I shifted Ember into a more comfortable position and lifted her head so that it rested on my thigh, not having anything better to cushion her with.

"She'll be all right in a few minutes," Nic said, shoulders easing. "Perhaps saddened to be awake, judging by the cheerful expression on her face, but otherwise all right. It was good that you found her, Dio."

I didn't reply. Finding her had nothing to do with me and everything to do with the others insisting I go after her. The knight put his hand on the bare skin of her ankle. I curled my free hand into a fist, the points of claws digging into my palm.

Before I could lose my ability to cope with his latest trespass, Ember sucked in a deep breath and her eyes fluttered open. She frowned, glancing around at all of us before sitting up.

"Did I fall asleep?"

"After a fashion," Nic answered her, then explained about the flowers.

Ember's eyes widened, and she let the knight wrap his arms around her. "I suppose Robby did say Dream was every bit as deadly as Nightmare."

154

Nic smiled. "In some ways more so. Nightmare rarely hides its danger behind a pretty façade."

"Only in the case of princes, right?" Ash laughed. "And the occasional attractive monster."

My brother chuckled. "Yes."

He was clearly comfortable with the current situation. Anger tightened my jaw.

"Anyone know where Robby went?" Ember glanced around the clearing.

"He's working on finding us transportation," Nic said.

Ember groaned and climbed to her feet, her knight assisting her. She leaned against him while she continued to recover from the blossoms.

The jester stepped out of nowhere and bowed in that sardonic way that only jesters could pull off and survive. "Your carriage awaits, princess."

Ember flipped the jester off, which really was the only acceptable answer to his behavior. It made me wonder if Ember had known him for some length of time. There was a lot I needed to catch up on.

"Aww, is that any way to treat an old friend?"

"It is when you ate all my espresso beans. Those were a gift from Geraint." Ember put her hands on her hips and glared at the jester, who smiled.

"You eat too many of them."

"You eat most of them." She jabbed him in the chest with her finger.

They had definitely known each other for a while. A different kind of pain than anger constricted my chest. I'd missed so much of Ember's life.

The jester offered Ember his arm, and she took it, laughing as he escorted her out of the clearing, her knight following and not looking bothered by seeing Ember on another man's arm. He wasn't sleeping with her, too, was he?

My brother walked over to me and put his hand on my shoulder. "Relax, Dio. They're just friends."

"Jesters don't have friends."

"This one does." Nic frowned for a moment, then shrugged. "At least as much as anyone in his position can have a friend."

I wondered what Nic was referring to but guessed he wouldn't answer. At least not right now.

Ash followed the trio, commenting on Geraint's ass or something else ridiculous.

"Are you going to be okay, Dio?"

I turned and looked at Nic. "I've missed so much."

"We both missed years of Ember's life. We need to make up for it now."

"But I loved her, and I wanted her, and now she barely knows me. You didn't even want her and now look at the two of you." I kicked at a clump of harmless flowers. The rock that had hidden in their midst did its best to break my toe. My brother ignored my swearing.

"It wasn't that I didn't want her, Dio. I simply wanted the unknown to remain unknown for a great deal longer. It's in my nature, if nothing else." Nic swirled into shadow for a moment, then solidified. "She will come around to you, Dio. You simply have to recognize it's her place to choose her lovers and accept Geraint."

"I don't know that I can," I admitted.

"Then Nightmare might fall, because it's going to take all of us together to stop whatever is happening, and it will take her creativity and mortal energy to help us recreate what is being erased, if we even can."

"No pressure or anything." I ran my hand through my hair and clenched my jaw.

Nic squeezed my shoulder then gestured. "We should get going. They may not wait for us."

"You trust the jester?"

"Yes."

"You're sure?"

"He is working in the best interests of Dream. He genuinely likes Ember and her knight, and currently our interests align. I trust him."

"For now," I finished his sentence for him.

"For now," Nic agreed.

My brother faded into the shadows as soon as we were amongst the trees and vanished, catching up to the others by shadow stepping. Grumbling, I forced my exhausted limbs to move faster and hurried after the others, wondering if I could do what Nic said. Could I share Ember with someone other than Nic and Baz if we ever found him?

I wanted to say that I could, for the good of Nightmare, if nothing else. Unfortunately, every instinct I had was telling me the knight was trespassing and that I should rip his throat out and watch his life bleed into the ground.

Warring with myself, I followed after the woman I loved and hoped I wouldn't screw things up further between us. Only time would tell.

Dakota Brown

CHAPTER 18

Ember

"Holy crap, that's a floating pirate ship!" I stopped and stared. A massive wooden hull eclipsed the vibrant blue sky. Several masts held sails that flapped loosely in a breeze I didn't feel.

"It's on loan from a friend," Robby said with a pleased grin.

"Are those cannons?"

"Yes, princess. Hopefully, we won't have to use them."

"You totally jinxed us."

The jester chuckled. "Possibly."

Casey came over to the railing and waved at us. A few beings moved around in the rigging. I didn't want to assume they were human just because they looked human shaped. This was Dream after all.

"The stained glass on the back is beautiful. Is that normal? Wouldn't it break in rough seas?" I shielded my eyes from the sun so I could get a better look.

"My dear, this is a dream ship," Robby reminded me.

"Right. I bet it's amazing inside."

"Yes. You'll love it."

"Um, how do we get up?" I looked around for a ladder to get us in the air.

"Unless you can fly or step through the shadows, you'll have to climb." Robby winked at me.

"Climb what?"

"Princess of Nightmare, surely you can come up with something." Robby stepped away from me, flourished a bow, and turned sideways, vanishing.

"Fucker," I muttered, but he was right. I needed to get used to using my powers. I hadn't touched them since I'd arrived. Instead, I'd gotten snared by an energy-eating patch of flowers that might have killed me.

I wasn't sure what Dio could climb, or if he even needed my help, but I knew Ash, Geraint, and I could all easily climb silks, so I called to the essence swirling through the air and pulled and shaped it until a pair of colorful pink silks tumbled from the railing of the pirate ship.

"How'd I make color?" I'd only ever managed black before. I had been able to alter the color of the dream clothing I'd worn, but I hadn't created the dream clothing in the first place.

"You're learning," Nic answered without truly answering. Maybe that was enough. I was learning. It hadn't been difficult, either.

Ash went over to the silks, reached up, and lifted herself, wrapping her feet and pushing upward. She sensuously climbed up to the top and swung a leg over the railing. Geraint glanced at me, and I gestured for him to go. Nothing would happen to me with Nic at my side.

"I will spot you," Nic said when Geraint was halfway up the silks I'd created.

Amazingly enough, I hadn't even considered the idea of falling. I knew I wasn't over my trauma, but I was well on my way to conquering it.

"Thank you." I gave Nic a quick kiss on the cheek before heading over to the silks once Geraint had thrown his leg over the railing.

"How are you getting up there, brother?" I heard Nic ask Dio as I started my climb, though I didn't hear his answer. Maybe I should have asked him if he wanted my help?

When I reached the section where the silks lay against the hull of the boat, I had to work a little harder to get around that, but all in all, it was an easy climb up. After I threw my leg over the railing and stood on the wooden deck, I looked back toward the ground. From up here, the height was dizzying. I gripped the smooth railing and watched as Nic wrapped Dio in his shadows and assisted him up the side. Since Nic had Dio under control, I banished the silks I'd created into wisps of dream essence and looked around at the flying pirate ship. Well, I didn't actually know it was a pirate ship, but I suspected it was. The ship didn't currently fly a flag.

A handful of dream folk scurried around as if getting ready to make sail—or I imagined that was what they were doing, anyway. Casey stood up on the captain's deck and waved at me, a big grin on her face. Ash had already gone up to join her. Geraint was casually exploring, though I got the impression he was making sure there were no hidden surprises.

I climbed the ladder that led up to the higher deck and joined Casey and Ash. Robby stood at the wheel, talking to another dream being, a woman wearing a tricorn hat, beige trousers, a white shirt, and a battered leather vest. Tattoos climbed her arms, and a parrot perched on her shoulder. She, like the rest of the crew, was barefoot. Her attitude told me she was in charge of the ship right now, maybe even the captain. Though since Robby had said the ship was on loan, the captain might not be present.

"This is really amazing," Casey said when I joined them. "I can't believe you're a princess."

"Ahh, yeah." I shrugged. "I can't believe it, either. This is all pretty crazy."

"Am I really stuck here?" Her voice fell.

"I think so," I said. "But one thing I want to do once we've fixed everything else is see if there's a way to get you and the other dreambound performers home."

"I think I'm okay with being stuck here," Casey whispered. "If you can't fix it, that is. Even if Robby tires of me, or I tire of him, I'll be able to make some sort of life here. It is a really cool place."

"It is." I glanced at Ash.

Her expression was blank, and I guessed she was trying to hide her own feelings about being stuck here. If she hadn't been engaged, maybe she'd feel differently. Maybe not. She loved being a lawyer.

My cousin went over to the railing and stared out into the distance. I let her have her space. We could talk when she was ready.

Nic and Dio joined us up on the deck. I went over to Nic's side and put my arm around him. His cool shadows swirled around us and he hugged me against him. After a quick glance at the bright sun, he pressed his lips to my temple before murmuring, "I'm going below."

"Are we ready?" Robby came over as Nic dissolved into shadows and sank through the decking.

Casey's eyes widened, and she stared at the floor where Nic had disappeared. "That's crazy."

"Yes, our shadowy prince is quite talented in dealing with the darker parts of the realm," Robby answered her.

I couldn't tell if he was being more serious or making some sort of pun, so I ignored him. "I'd say we're ready on our end, but I don't know anything about boats, especially flying ones."

"Ahh, dear princess, this mighty ship." He emphasized the last word. "Will sail as soon as we are ready."

"Then we're ready. Where are we going?"

"We are seeking forgotten dreams, and Baz. Once we've located him, we'll head to Dream Palace."

"You make it sound so easy." I hugged myself.

"It will take a bit of searching, but I have a destination in mind." Robby bowed to me, ignored Dio, and offered his arm to Casey, leading her back toward the ship's wheel.

"Is he always like that?" Dio glared after the jester.

"Robby? Yeah." I shrugged. "You get used to it after a while, and he's a fantastic manager."

Dio's brows furrowed. "Manager of what?"

"Robby did most of the sales aspects of our business. Finding us gigs, arranging our contracts and travel, accommodations, things like that. He also helps set up our portable rig and runs the lift if we need it."

"I take it you've known Robby for a while, then?" He ran a hand through his curly hair and sighed.

I wanted to go to him, comfort him, though I wasn't sure what bothered him. I didn't know this version of Dio well enough to guess. He sagged against the railing overlooking the rest of the ship.

"What's wrong?"

He shook his head. "I'm not sure. It's as if my limbs have no energy."

"Well, you were torn apart for like ten years. It might take some time to recover from that." I joined him, leaning my forearms on the railing.

Dio was significantly taller than I was, with broad shoulders that looked like he'd once carried a great deal of lean muscle. I could almost see him as the winged panther his essence had appeared to us as. Powerful, lithe, stalking through the forest or grasslands after prey. He'd always loved playing tag and any other game of chase as a kid.

All three of them had been playful. Nic had always been a bit more serious and reserved, Dio more assertive, and Baz had been eager to please. A total opposite of how not-Baz had treated us.

"Maybe," Dio replied after a minute. "I feel it might be something more."

"What made you separate yourself from your essence?"

"Honestly, I don't remember. This was after Baz had gone crazy and kicked us out of Nightmare Castle. Nic and I fled, and we chose to separate so we could help as many of the beings in Nightmare as we could. That went well enough, though it became difficult to keep in contact with each other.

"Then one day, some of Baz's creatures came after me. They shouldn't have been able to overpower a prince, but they were more than I could handle, and I fled, worried that if they got me, they'd drain my essence. I know I fled to the conscious realm, but the rest is foggy." He fell silent for a moment, staring at his clasped hands. "I'm sure I thought it was a good idea. It might even have been necessary. I don't know how I managed it, and I certainly would never do it again."

"Maybe you need more energy. I know how to syphon it. Maybe I can give some back to you? If you want me to try."

Dio tightened his jaw as he thought, then glanced to the lower part of the ship. His eyes narrowed when he saw Geraint, and he shook his head.

"No, best not." He turned and left before I could say anything else.

Well, fine, if he didn't want me to try to help him, I wouldn't.

164

The breeze picked up, and the deck tilted, distracting me from my thoughts.

The sails snapped in the wind before catching and filling with air. They billowed and the ship slowly built speed. Breath catching in my throat with wonder as the ground fell away below us, I stared, awestruck.

Dream viewed from the air reminded me of a fantasy painting, all bright colors and beautiful settings. I couldn't wait to explore the land more in depth.

As I watched, I noticed some areas that were smudged out, as if someone had taken an eraser to them. The ship turned to avoid one such area. That someone had caused these nothingness storms and was erasing the beauty broke my heart. Even Nightmare was beautiful in its way, and it had been hit even harder.

We sailed for hours, and the sun progressed rapidly across the sky toward the far horizon. Then we seemed to cross some sort of invisible line and the sun rose again, sliding backward. What the hell? I'd been able to ignore the fast movement of the sun, knowing how dreams often went, but the backward flow was a little too much. I climbed down the ladder and went into the big cabin in search of Nic.

The stained glass caught my attention before I could see if my lover was here. Technically, we were married, but I couldn't think of him as my husband. Despite the game having binding consequences we hadn't even remotely thought possible, it had just been a game.

I walked farther into the room, hand outstretched, though I wouldn't touch. The sun lit the colored glass and cast an epic reflection on the thick rug that covered the floor. The scenes, all fanciful ocean images such as mermaids, narwhals, fish with tridents clutched in their fins, seemed to move across the rug as the boat turned and the angle of the sun changed.

"It's quite beautiful, isn't it?"

I turned. Nic had sprawled in an actual bed and stared at me. I wondered if I had woken him.

"It's amazing. This entire room is amazing. Were you up all night?"

He nodded. "I usually am." He patted the bed next to himself.

I took the invitation and went over, sitting so I faced him. He ran his fingers lightly over my thigh.

"Are you all right?" He traced light circles over my leg.

"I'm okay. Worried about Ash. Worried about Casey. Worried about Dio and Geraint."

Nic tugged on my sleeve, and I let him pull me over until I was laying down with my back to his chest. He wrapped tendrils of shadows around my ankles and put his leg over mine until we were spooned tightly together. I lay my head on his arm and ran my fingers lightly over the exposed skin of his wrist.

The soft touch of his fingers running over my body as he caressed me while he held me soothed away some of the tension.

"There's only so much we can do about any of that right now, luv. Dio understands the consequences of hurting you. He won't harm Geraint."

"Yeah, but he's obviously not happy about my knight, and if we're supposed to be together..."

"Ember, as you've said, it's your life and your choice."

"But Nightmare?"

"There's much we need to discover about this destruction. I know Robby thinks the key to stopping this is all of us being together, but I believe it's deeper than that. The Dream princesses still don't have their partner, after all. Ideally, you will choose to be with all of us, yes, but we have time for that. Let's focus on finding Baz and figuring out how to stop this plot against Dream. Then we will see what can be done to help Ash and Casey."

"One thing at a time, right?"

"One thing at a time, princess."

I fell silent, enjoying the soft touch of his fingers running over my shoulder, down my arm, through my hair, tracing a gentle line on my cheek. I also enjoyed the way tendrils of shadow twisted up my legs, holding me. Feeling safe and secure, I lay there and listened to the creak of the ship as we soared through the air.

"Everything will work out," Nic murmured, and I let myself believe him.

***

"Ember?" Geraint's gentle touch and familiar musical lilt woke me later.

I hadn't realized I'd fallen asleep in Nic's arms, but I woke feeling rested and safe. He'd pulled a blanket over me at some point.

"Hey," I answered sleepily.

"Sorry to bother you two, but we're nearing the first stop Robby wants to make."

I stretched out my hand and grasped Geraint's. "Thank you, Knight."

"Anything for you, Spark."

I grinned.

"Is that infernal sun still up?" Nic grumbled, stirring awake.

"It is." Geraint glanced over at the stained glass, still aglow with sunlight.

The prince sighed. "Fucking Dream."

Spreading my arms out, I deliberately wiggled my butt against Nic as I stretched. He chuckled and wrapped me in his shadow tentacles.

"I don't get the sense we have time for distractions," he murmured.

Geraint brushed some of my hair out of my eyes. "No," he agreed with Nic. "But we can enjoy thinking about later."

"Torture, you mean," I grumbled and snuggled back into Nic's embrace.

My prince kissed my neck. "Come on. If I can deal, you certainly can."

"But someone has me all tied up," I replied. "I couldn't get up even if I wanted to, and this bed is really soft."

One of the two of them pulled the warm blanket off me, and with a teasing caress, Nic's tentacles withdrew.

I deliberately moaned as he teased me. Both Geraint and Nic stared at me. The prince flicked his tongue across his lips and my knight cleared his throat.

Someone banged on the door, startling all three of us.

"Let's go!" Robby shouted.

I laughed and rolled out of bed. Geraint took my arm and helped me to my feet. I raised up on my toes and gave him a quick kiss. Nic flowed out of bed, more shadow than man, and reformed next to me.

We left the spacious cabin, and I spared a moment to glare at a smirking Robby before I went and looked over the side.

The ship hovered just over the ground in another lush, grassy field. Colorful wildflowers mixed with the grass, and a herd of deer foraged in the distance. A herd of familiar white horses grazed nearby.

"Are we riding?" I couldn't wait to ride one of the horses with the silver hooves again.

"For a little while, then we have to go on foot. Wise dream creatures avoid the forgotten dreams," Robby answered.

"What does that make us?" Ash joined us at the railing, running her hand over the smooth wood.

"Certainly not wise," Robby replied. "Desperate, however, does describe the situation."

"All right, Spark. Do your thing so we can get down." Ash gestured toward the ground.

I touched her arm, and she glanced at me, flashing a quick smile. "It'll be all right, Ember. We'll figure out how I feel about all this once the realm is safe, okay?"

"Okay." I turned my attention to the dream essence that permeated the environment and pulled on it, thinking of teal silks this time. In moments, a set of fabrics tumbled to the ground, attached at the railing and the most perfect shade of teal I'd ever seen.

Ash shook her head in awe. "Well done, Ember. Maybe if I can develop some kick-ass skills like that, I won't hate it here after all."

I grinned at her. "Yeah. We'll work on that for sure."

Geraint went first, climbing over the side and down the silks. I noticed someone had given him a sword, and he had it slung over his back.

Ash went next, then Casey. Dio followed, lowering himself carefully. I noticed Nic watching his brother closely. Dio wavered a little at the bottom, but no one was brave enough to try to help him keep his feet. Nic stepped into the shadows, but Dio was recovered by the time Nic appeared next to him.

When it was my turn, I confidently stepped over the rail and lowered myself. I considered the fear that not-Baz had instilled in me while I went down, but my limbs didn't freeze up, and I wasn't shaking by the time I'd gotten to the bottom. My ability to control the silks and the situation gave me confidence. Yes, Nic would catch me if I fell, but really, I could catch myself.

I knew I was grinning when I joined the others, but no one commented on it.

The horses with the silver hooves that chimed like bells when they rang on stone came over, each selecting a rider. Nic helped me mount before assisting Dio.

I patted the warm neck of the horse who'd chosen to carry me. "Thank you."

He flipped his head, acknowledging my words.

"I think I've dreamed of these horses," Ash said, wiping at her eye. "They might have saved my life."

The horse Ash rode curled his head around and lipped at her foot. Ash rubbed his neck.

I looked away, letting my cousin have her moment.

Once the others were mounted, Robby took the lead and we set off at a ground-eating pace. Though I didn't know how to ride, as before, some magic of the realm kept me tightly mounted and I could relax into the horse's motion and enjoy the experience.

The landscape we traversed gradually changed from lush green to a dryer grassland environment and when we reached the edge of the grasses, the horses stopped, none of them setting foot beyond the abrupt boundary between sand and grass.

"We walk from here," Robby said.

I thanked my mount with a pat and slid off his back. He nuzzled me before turning to join the other horses. Their silver hooves flashed as they trotted away.

The desolate landscape ahead was so at odds with everything else I'd seen in Dream that I shivered. "We're going there?"

"Yes, Princess. The forgotten dreams are forgotten for a reason. Often, they bleed into nightmares and change location, but some are simply things humans no longer dream of for whatever reason." Robby took a step onto the sand.

"What is this one?"

"I don't know. We'll find out once we get into it."

I followed the jester. The sand crunched strangely under my feet as if it were dried up and forgotten and not quite real sand any longer.

Nic came up alongside me, and Dio flanked me on the other side. Casey and Ash trailed behind us. Geraint moved to follow and watch our backs.

"Do we have to worry about, like, sand worms or anything, here?" A few popular movies from years back surfaced in my mind.

"We're in Dream, Princess. Those sorts of terrors are unlikely. If we were in Nightmare, yes." Robby was a *fantastic* tour guide.

I shook my head and put my energy into walking and studying my surroundings. Ahead, the air seemed blurry, but not quite in the same way as the places that had been erased by the nothingness storms.

"That's the boundary," Nic explained. "Forgotten Nightmares, should they have enough strength to linger, have similar outlines. When Dream or Nightmare creatures enter these forgotten places, they risk being dissolved, as there is no belief left in the dream. It sucks the essence out of the creatures that enter."

"Oh, great, so, like, us humans have to go in on our own?" Ash caught onto the implications before I did.

"No. Robby, Dio, and I can protect ourselves, and Geraint's supply of belief is unlimited as long as he is around Ember. I suspect he is also nearly as mortal as you are and won't have issues. If he does, I'll make sure he gets out," Nic swirled into shadow before solidifying.

I had to trust Nic, but I wasn't feeling terribly reassured. Still, when Robby pushed into the blurry barrier between the living dreams and the forgotten ones I followed.

On the other side, I stopped and stared.

"What the fuck?" Ash breathed, giving voice to my thoughts.

I frowned, staring at what looked to be a perfect model neighborhood laid out before us. The houses were nearly identical, but different shades of cheerful pastels, and a few here and there had brick facade. Each house had an identical white picket fence, a perfectly manicured lawn, a single old-style sedan in the driveway, and most yards had evidence of children. Balls or bikes, or other toys laying in the yards. A few houses had front porch swings. The sky was blue without a cloud to be seen, and the sun shone overhead.

I didn't see any people, but if this was a forgotten dream, that didn't surprise me.

"It'll take hours to search this," Ash said.

"Then we'd best start." Robby set off.

I glanced back at Geraint. He hastened to my side, rubbing his arms.

"You all right?"

"Yeah. The air feels dead. It's better near you."

I put my hand in his and we headed for the first house.

Casey paired up with Robby, Ash reluctantly took Dio as a partner, and Nic flitted from shadow to shadow. Though there weren't many in this seemingly idyllic suburban neighborhood.

"This is creepy," Geraint said as we walked up the driveway. "I can't imagine what thoughts gave this sort of dream life, let alone forgot it."

"Yeah." I pushed open the front door. It wasn't locked. The ghost of an echo of laughing children and the crackle of a static then a vaguely familiar music jingle

172

teased my ears before vanishing into the dull silence that filled this space.

No birds called. No sounds or car noises or anything filled the background.

The living room had an old-style boxy television with tuning knobs and antenna. A green curved couch sat in front of the TV, and an armchair sat beside a large radio. The rest of the house was similar, really old-style appliances that looked brand new, an ironing board with an iron on it, white pressed collared shirts, a frilly flowered apron hung in the kitchen. One bedroom had bunk beds and pictures of old airplanes. Another bedroom had a small kid's bed all in pinks, with stuffed animals everywhere. The master bedroom was laid out like it was from a sitcom.

"Sixties?" I guessed hesitantly.

Geraint shook his head. "Fifties, I think, based on the car out front and the radio."

"Huh. What kind of dream was this?"

Ash and Dio wandered into the bedroom where we looked around, mystified.

"The American dream," Ash supplied.

I had to wrack my brain to think about what that even meant. What had the American dream been? This?

"Everyone dreamed of having the perfect home and all the newest conveniences," Ash said. "We learned about it in school, remember? We'd just come out of the Second World War, and industry was booming. It's been a long time since anything like this has been achievable or perhaps even desirable, and I guess the dream's been forgotten. There were a lot of problems with this dream, too. Equality wasn't a thing, for starters."

A thought tickled at the back of my mind about other concerns in the fifties, but that era had happened so long ago I almost didn't even remember learning about it in school.

"Right. Some weird segregation shit or something, right?"

Ash nodded. "We've come a long way since then. Still a long way to go, though."

"Yeah," I agreed with my cousin. Ash was a lot more in touch with the day-to-day inequalities that people dealt with both legally and in general both from her own personal experiences and as a lawyer. I didn't think that was what was bothering me about this era, though. Maybe it would come to me.

"Are all the houses like this?" I asked.

Ash shrugged. "I imagine so, but we've only checked two. Let's keep looking."

Geraint stayed close. He was right. The air did feel dead. There were hints of Dream essence but not nearly what I'd become used to. Even the conscious realm had more than this.

I looked at Dio. He'd been studying me, but quickly glanced away, sparing a quick glare for Geraint before he headed out of the creepy house.

He and Ash split off again, and we went from house to house, looking for some clue as to where Baz might be. Nic touched base. His search was going well, if more slowly than he could have accomplished in a realm filled with the normal levels of essence, and he found more of the same. Robby and Casey reported the same results.

Trying to ignore the anxious, yet hopeless feeling that dragged at my feet and weighed down my shoulders, I trudged to yet another house.

A ball rolled down the driveway, bumping into my feet. Idly I kicked it into the grass and went to the front door, Geraint on my heels.

It didn't occur to me that the moving ball was the first true difference I'd seen in this place until the door slammed shut behind me, cutting me off from my knight. He pounded on the door, but it didn't budge.

"Well, look at you."

The harsh voice full of venom sent my heart racing.

I spun around.

CHAPTER 19

Ember

"Who the hell are you?"

I stared at the woman who lounged on a seriously old school fainting couch. It didn't match the rest of the fifties' décor, but then, neither did she. The woman was probably older than me by about ten years and wore an elegant gown and smoked a cigarette on the end of a long stick. I wrinkled my nose at the smell. This house was clearly fifties era, but her clothing made me think of the twenties. She had her brown hair done up, and I thought it might be longer based on the intricate style.

She stood and sauntered over to me, moving languorously, like a cat taunting a mouse.

"Who am I? Honey, I'm just a woman who wants to get home."

"Home?"

"The conscious realm. Manhattan, to be specific." She circled me, and I tried not to sneeze at the unfamiliar odor of cigarette smoke. Most places were smokeless these days.

"You're dreambound?"

She nodded, wandered back to her fainting chair, and draped herself back into it. "I was going to be a star. Instead, I've been trapped here for countless years."

"You know, if it's been that long, you might consider staying here." I backed until I pressed against the door. The handle wouldn't turn when I tried it. Geraint had stopped beating on the door. I hoped like hell he was searching for another way in.

"I'm quite certain I'll find my place in Hollywood, regardless of the era."

I raised my eyebrows, but I wasn't about to dash her dreams. I was also a performer, after all.

"Well, I know a few other folks who are stuck here. As soon as we figure out how to stop the nothingness storms, I'm going to try and find a way to send them home." I tried the door again.

The woman burst out laughing. "Oh, aren't you pure and sweet? When the Dream realm is erased, there will be nothing to hold me here. I'll be able to return."

"Or you might be erased with the rest of Dream," I pointed out.

"Mortals are not affected. I tested it on another dreambound. He was fine."

"Where is he now?"

She waved her hand as if it were inconsequential. "No idea. He wandered off, as everyone does after a while. Eternity in this insane landscape grows tiresome."

"Oh." She caused the nothingness storms? "How'd you do it?"

The woman shrugged one elegantly exposed shoulder. "Nightmare beings not content with the status quo, a potion allowing me to dream powerfully, and a great deal of energy and intention. It took a while for everything to line up, and I have a few things left to do."

"Like?"

She grinned. "You'll find out. Now, if you'll excuse me." She stood, patting the back of the couch. "The fainting couch is quite comfortable, by the way."

While I stared, wondering why the woman switched topics, she headed to the back of the house.

Before I could even think to rush forward and stop her, she was in the kitchen and the walls melded together, leaving me no way out.

"What? Wait!" I slammed my hand against the wall. Drywall would have given to my attack, but whatever she'd done to the inside of this house had turned it as hard as stone.

"Fuck." I shook out my hand, wincing. "Nic!" I shouted with my mind and my voice. I ran to the window and pulled back the curtains just as Geraint swung a baseball bat at it. The bat shattered, the glass remained unharmed.

I slammed my hands against the window. "Geraint!"

"I'm going to find Nic."

I couldn't hear him, but I could read his lips and I nodded.

Just then, sirens pierced the silence. Those, I could hear, and suddenly I remembered what else had plagued the fifties. The threat of nuclear war.

Geraint looked up at the sky, then back at me, eyes wide.

"Shit!" I threw a chair at the glass and narrowly avoided getting brained by it as it bounced back at me.

Geraint held up a finger and ran off out of view.

"No, no, no..." Apparently getting rid of me was on the woman's to-do list. I suspected an atomic blast in a forgotten dream would be devastating enough that I wouldn't survive it. The American dream might be forgotten, but nearly the entire world knew what happened when a nuclear weapon exploded.

Geraint returned with the others. I put my hands on the window. Nic attacked the glass, but it resisted the

179

tendrils of shadow he used to try to drain the creation of its power.

Ash shouted and pointed to the sky. Robby held Casey. Geraint attacked the window with his sword, and Dio went crazy, throwing himself at the glass with hands partially shifted into paws with dagger-like talons.

I even tried draining the essence from this side with no success.

Geraint put his hands on the glass, and I touched mine to his, the barrier preventing us from making physical contact.

Nic placed his next to Geraint's.

"Fucking go!" I pointed away from me when Ash danced around, urgently gesturing toward the sky. Dio grabbed Nic, and they argued before Dio shoved Nic away.

"I love you," Nic mouthed at me before grabbing Geraint and racing away.

Geraint had a second to fight the prince before I gestured for him to leave. Nic wrapped my knight in shadows and dragged him away. Robby, Casey, and Ash took off after them.

Dio looked up at the sky, then put his hands on the window. I mirrored him on the other side of the glass. I could see what Ash had been pointing at. The air raid sirens continued their howl, and several bombs fell toward our location, dream logic providing me with a detailed view I wouldn't have in the conscious realm.

"Ember," he mouthed. "Try to ride the shadows."

I shut my eyes and focused. We were still in Dream, not Nightmare, as far as I could tell. In dreams, there were always ways to save the day. I wasn't sure why Dio had stayed and Nic had left. He'd had to force Geraint to leave me. They had to have had a good reason, and I was glad they were gone. It was going to be hard enough to save me and Dio.

Gritting my teeth, I grabbed for the meager amounts of dream essence still present in this collapsing, forgotten fantasy of a lost age. There wasn't much, but I got it to respond. I shoved the essence at the window, burrowing through the middle, making a hole.

"Ember, go!" Dio shouted at me when he saw what I was doing.

Ignoring him, I put my hands in the slowly widening hole in the glass and pulled. Dio gave me an exasperated look, then shoved his hands in next to mine, claws out, and tore at the glass.

This time, we made progress. Not fast enough for me to get out, but it was enough to break the containment the crazy dreambound lady had put on the room. I grabbed Dio's hands just as the bombs touched down.

Shutting my eyes against the impossibly bright explosion, I mentally claimed Dio as my own and yanked him into the shadows with me. I didn't have time to think of a destination, clinging to the thought of ending up at the same place the rest of the people I had claimed in this crazy realm.

My body dissolved into shadow, dragging Dio along as the explosion washed through where we'd stood, obliterating the crumbling dream as we escaped into nothing. The thin thread connecting me to Dio was strong as we were touching, and I found the threads pulling me toward my friends and lovers. There was another weak tendril of connection, and I latched onto it instead of returning to those I knew. I wasn't sure what made me do it, but it felt right.

Our location shifted drastically, and we seemed to land right as I lost my hold on the shadows. My body spasmed as it reformed, and I went sprawling across cold tile. Bile rose in my throat, but I kept from vomiting all over the place.

Someone groaned, and I forced my eyes open. Dio lay not far from me, hands now fully human again. He heaved, but also kept whatever he'd last eaten from coming up.

"Please never do that again," he moaned.

"Save your life?" I struggled to my knees, staring at the floor as the room spun around me.

"Yank me through the shadows," Dio clarified.

"Right, next time you're about to get nuked, I'll leave you to it." I leaned forward and pressed my forehead to the cool tile, willing the world to stop. Hopefully, we weren't about to be attacked by anything.

"We couldn't all leave you," Dio said. "And I am the weakest link right now. I knew you'd get out if someone gave you the right idea. I didn't think you'd be able to take me with you."

"Don't complain, then," I grumbled.

"I'll stop complaining when the world stops spinning." Dio clutched his head.

I snorted.

"I didn't even think that was possible. Nic has never been able to do it."

"Yeah, well, don't get too excited. I have no idea where we're at."

My equilibrium settled, and I sat up. I could no longer sense that weak thread of connection I had followed to get here, and I wasn't about to go back into the shadows to find it. We could look around the old-fashioned way.

"We have to be in Nightmare." I shivered as I took in the flickering lighting overhead, more of the long florescent bulbs burned out than worked. The buzz of the working lights was loud and irritating now that I was paying attention. The walls were concrete blocks, once painted some sort of pastel green, but now mostly chipped off or discolored with mildew. Random stainless-steel trays glittered dully in the weird lighting, and debris littered the floor.

"Hospital?" I guessed.

Dio made it to his knees and looked around. "Looks like it. Horror movie version anyway. We're definitely in Nightmare."

"Is it strange that I'm kind of glad to be back here?"

Dio chuckled. "I feel the same way, though I do like Dream. Very pretty and all."

"The others made it out of the decaying forgotten dream, right?" I could still feel my connection to Nic, so I assumed that meant he had, but I had to ask.

"Yeah." Dio struggled to his feet, leaning on one of the metal trays to catch his balance.

"You okay?"

He shook his head but otherwise didn't answer, and I let it go.

"Why are we here?" he asked instead of answering me.

"I followed a thread of connection that felt similar to the one I have with you. I thought maybe we'd find Baz."

A dark notion flickered through my thoughts. Had that really been my reason, or had I been afraid my friends weren't safe and I'd only shadow walk myself into the blast if I went to them? No, I'd been thinking of Baz. That nasty thought hadn't surfaced until Dio had questioned me. I shivered.

"This place feels as empty as the other."

"We're in a forgotten Nightmare. It has a little more substance than the dream we just left, so I suspect this one has a few mortals still sending it energy. But it's not long for the realm. At least in its current state."

"We should look around, see if we find Baz or something else important." I offered Dio my hand.

After a small hesitation, he accepted, his hand smooth and warm when he grasped mine.

"I've missed you," he admitted.

"I've only remembered that you three existed for a few weeks, but I've missed the time we could have had together now that I remember."

He squeezed my hand, and we picked a direction to explore. Straight through a set of heavy metal doors. Hallways stretched out to either side, fading into blackness, but the metal doors were in full detail, and I suspected the dream ended not far into the shadows.

We pushed through the double doors together, him opening one, me the other. We stopped on the other side and stared.

The room was large, gymnasium style. Row after row of large cylindrical machines held above the ground by metal supports filled the room.

"What the hell are those?" I breathed, a chill trailing down my spine.

Dio's hand tightened on mine. "Iron lungs."

It took me a few minutes to remember what those were, then a shudder wracked my body. "A lifesaving nightmare, but holy crap."

"Well, let's see if we can find Baz." Dio tugged on my hand, and we made our way through the nightmare polio ward.

The banks of iron lungs seemed to stretch forever, but eventually we reached the end of one row. We turned and walked another. Hours passed us, feeling like an eternity and no time at all.

"Dio, what are we going to do?" I turned another corner.

"About?"

"Us."

"Oh." He ran his free hand through his curls. "We don't have to do anything."

I stopped and faced him. "I can feel your energy waning, especially in this mostly forgotten dream. You're not completely you."

"And you think sex will help that?" he bit out, though he didn't take his hand from mine. "I'm not even sure I have the energy for that." The last, he said more quietly.

"I meant letting me see if I can give you some more energy. We don't need to have sex for that. One of the first things I had to learn was how to syphon Nic's energy, and I've since learned to feed it back to him."

Dio raised his hand and made as if to brush his fingers along my cheek before he let it fall to his side. "I can't."

"Fine. Let's finish searching and get out of here." I dropped his hand and hurried away, knowing he would follow.

The scuff of our shoes on the tile, soft thuds, and the occasional squeak, were the only sounds other than our breathing in this tomb-like ward. The machines were silent, long since they'd been needed, and the nightmare didn't include any other audible elements in this room.

Toward the middle in the back, I noticed one of the iron lungs seemed to be occupied. I hurried over. Conflicting emotions tightened my chest as I caught sight of the occupant. Fear as I saw my tormentor's face, softened in sleep, overlaid with my memories of Baz as a kid. This being wasn't responsible for not-Baz's behavior.

"How do we get him out?"

Dio already inspected the contraption that encased Baz's body. He manipulated a lever and a soft hiss sounded. He was able to pull the iron lung apart, and together we figured out how to remove the collar around Baz's neck. Then we were left with an unconscious Nightmare prince.

"Now what?" I sighed.

Dio shoved Baz's shoulder. "Wake up, sleepyhead."

Baz didn't move, body limp and unresponsive other than a slight rise and fall of his chest.

"He's alive, right?" I put my hand on his chest, confirming that I could feel what my eyes told me, that he was breathing.

"Yeah. Whatever is causing all this is probably making him sleep, too."

Oh, right. I'm the only one who knows. I was about to fill Dio in when the ground shuddered under us.

"We should get out of here." I grabbed the edge of the gurney that Baz lay on and Dio grabbed one side. We ran for the door, the clatter of the wheels across the tile loud. Before we could get to the other end of the ward, the world melted.

"Fuck!" I skidded to a halt, jerking the bed back in the other direction. The leading edge of the nothingness storm was too close. There was no way we would make it.

"Go through the shadows, Ember," Dio demanded.

Could I do it again? The real question was, did I have a choice? I didn't. Before Dio could stop me, I lunged across Baz's body and grabbed Dio's arm. The power came more easily to me this time, and I yanked Baz and Dio into the shadows. Latching onto the stronger connection I shared with Nic, I hurled the three of us away from the nothingness storm and prayed I could hold on long enough to get us safe with Nic and the others.

Pain tore at my mind, would have torn at my body if I had one. I was no stranger to pain. My chosen profession involved a great deal of physical discomfort and sometimes outright pain, but this was a whole new level of agony. Every molecule of my body screamed in protest as it tried to reform in a realm that couldn't support a physical body.

Screaming into the void, I held on as long as I could. This time, when my body coalesced, I lost the contents of my stomach before I lost consciousness.

CHAPTER 20

Dio

"**I**f I never have to do this again, it'll be too soon." I groaned, forehead pressed to the cool floor, curled up into as much of a ball as I could manage while the world heaved around me.

Ember had undoubtably saved my life again. I hoped there wasn't a next time.

"Ember! Dio!" Nic shouted.

"Is she okay?" I forced out when I saw feet in my peripheral vision.

"Unconscious," the damn knight said. "I think she'll be all right, though."

I heard clothing shift and assumed he was picking her up.

"Are you all right? Where did you find Baz?" Nic kneeled next to me and put his hand on my shoulder.

"I don't know how you do it, brother," I said instead of answering. "Your body being ripped apart all the time?"

"I am the shadow, Dio. It's different for me. Though the shadow realm takes some getting used to. It can be very disorienting," Nic replied.

"I remember them giving you some sort of special lessons when they saw you step through the shadows the first time." It was easier to focus on the memories than on the way my body screamed at me.

"Yes. The shadow people were generous with their knowledge." His voice was flat, and he didn't elaborate.

Nic had never spoken about his time with the shadow folk other than to tell us he didn't want to talk about it. Baz and I had speculated that it hadn't been pleasant, but that was the case for much of Nightmare.

"How's Baz?"

"Also unconscious."

Feeling a little better, I sat up on my knees. I wasn't shocked to find us in Dream Palace. I thought I'd recognized the pearlescent granite floors under my face. Not that I'd spent much time that up close and personal with them, but I'd certainly had my fair share of times to stare at them while being scolded.

As I'd suspected, the knight had taken my princess. A couple of Dream attendants lifted Baz onto a litter.

The jester and his mortal hung back and watched, and I didn't see Ember's cousin. Maybe she'd gone with the knight.

"How are you feeling?" Nic asked again.

"Like shit."

He helped while I climbed to my feet. "You're lucky to be alive to feel like shit," Nic pointed out with a smile.

I nodded and quickly regretted it. The world lurched.

"Go take care of your princess," I said to Nic when he let go of my arm. "I haven't been gone so long that I don't know the way to my room."

The weight of Nic's stare felt heavy on my shoulders as I got my bearings and headed toward a place I could rest. When I turned the corner, I looked back. He was staring at me, more solid than not because of all the light in Dream palace, a frown marring his brow.

I looked away and headed for my room. I needed a significant amount of sleep before I decided what to do next.

***

A solid stretch of rest had me feeling better, but far from good. I threw back the covers on my bed and reflected that my room, the suite that connected me to my brother's rooms, and their accommodations were probably the only darkly decorated places in the entire palace. The Nightmare queen's rooms might also be dark, but I'd never been in them.

The rest of the palace was all rainbows and unicorn farts, and normally I enjoyed visiting for a few days and getting a different view than the darker muted colors of Nightmare, but I was always glad to get home.

Home. The land that was being erased, and we didn't even know why or how. The need to go home gripped me. Without the mirrors to travel through, it would take longer to get there. It was possible I'd recovered enough to fully shift into my other form. I'd try once I was free of the palace and the city that surrounded it. The Dream beings freaked out a little when Nightmare creatures stalked through their pristine white streets.

I got up, took a minute to clean up in the human-style bathroom and exchange my conscious realm clothing for some created of Nightmare essence so I could change it at will. Also, it would resist actual damage, and the conscious realm stuff was beginning to smell. I left my old clothing on the ground and headed for the kitchen to ease my grumbling stomach. Then I'd leave.

The only people I encountered were the palace staff, beings crafted from Dream, wearing the sparkly rainbow tabards of the royal livery. They hurried about on their duties.

I let myself into the kitchen. I'd spent a lot of time here as a kid. Nic didn't eat a lot but Baz and I had devoured everything in sight and come back for more when they'd let us.

The staff recognized me, of course, and even acted pleased to see me. I suffered through the small talk with a smile. Normally, I wouldn't have minded. I just wanted to get away now. Away from the place where my princess was. The princess I couldn't have.

Why had they kept us from her after they'd found out we'd accidentally bound ourselves to her? Why had the knight overstepped? And why had I separated myself from my essence instead of going to Ember once I was in the conscious realm? Those questions plagued me while I tried to eat.

I clenched my fist, appetite gone. Shoving the last of the food down my throat took most of my energy. I made my way out of the kitchen, forcing out a few more pleasantries, before I stalked toward the nearest exit. I couldn't be sure because he didn't say anything, but I thought I sensed Nic watching me from the shadows.

The guards at the side door I chose didn't question me, simply opened the door. I walked out into the beautiful gardens that surrounded Dream Palace. It took everything I had not to stomp an ugly path through the colorful blooms. I was an adult. I wasn't going to have a tantrum. At least not where anyone could see it.

I barely paid attention to town, and as soon as I reached the wilds beyond, I sank down to my knees and forced my tired body into one last change. My feline shape reluctantly emerged. A brief rest gave me enough energy to trot away, but not enough to stretch my wings. Maybe when I got back to Nightmare, I'd be able to reclaim my former abilities and powers. Until then, I'd do the best I could. Alone. Because there was no way I could accept someone other than one of my brothers touching my mate.

CHAPTER 21

Geraint

I brushed my hand through my spark's hair and watched the gentle rise and fall of her chest. She slept deeply. Nic assured me he thought she was simply resting from overdoing it. I suspected he was right. Still, I sat in a heavily cushioned chair next to the bed in this opulent room Robby claimed belonged to the Nightmare Princess.

The décor was much darker in this room than in most of the rest of the palace: heavy woods, darker tones of colors, fitting for someone who was of the conscious realm, but also Nightmare.

As if summoned by my thoughts, the shadow prince swirled into existence next to me.

"Still asleep," Nic observed, sitting on the bed next to her and putting his hand on her leg.

"Yes."

"Dio left," Nic said with a sigh.

"Why?"

Nic stared at me for a moment, raising an eyebrow.

Dio didn't like me, but except at the beginning, he'd mostly avoided me. Though I supposed he'd been avoiding Ember, too. Shit.

"So what do we do?"

Nic shrugged. "Go after him, I suppose. I had hoped Ember had woken, so she could do it. I'll have to go."

"Why don't you let me do it? Sure, he hates me and all, but having two of you at risk, especially since we don't know what's wrong with Baz, is not the best idea. Also, you can stay here and hopefully feed Ember some energy to help revive her."

"Do you think you can track him?"

"I'm an aerialist," I pointed out. "Not a forest ranger. The only reason I have fighting skills is because I was created with them. They neglected to add bloodhound into the mix."

The prince actually smiled.

"I was hoping you could help with finding Dio," I added.

Nic shut his eyes while he thought, swirling into shadow, before reforming. "I can see if one of the dire wolves is available, or another being with scenting capabilities. They could do the tracking for you."

"That's a good plan."

"He won't be happy to see you," Nic said.

"No, but he's still pretty weak, as much as he's trying to hide it. I'm not worried about him hurting me. I'm worried about him getting hurt."

"I am, too. Stay with her while I find assistance for you."

Not that I had been intending to leave Ember alone, but I nodded, accepting the order, and taking her hand in mine. I gently caressed the smooth skin on the back of her hand while I waited for Nic to return.

***

I had always known I was from the dream realms, though I remembered little from my brief time here after I'd been created. A flash of memory of the young princes was all I had of them as children. That and some of

Ember's sketches. We were not introduced, but the ones who had created me had let me observe them from a distance for a time. I didn't even clearly remember the ones who had made me. My first actual memories were of meeting Ember. Her confident smile. Her grace. Her acceptance of a seemingly foreign—because of my accent—student with no parents. I would have protected her, regardless, but her friendship had made it that much easier.

She'd had a few close calls that I had kept her safe from through the years, that she knew nothing about. I didn't intend to tell her, either. She knew I protected her, and now she knew why, and so far, everything was working out. Unfortunately, protecting her, and Nightmare, meant going after one of her reluctant princes.

Ember had made it very clear that she wouldn't give me up, and I appreciated that, deeply and with all my heart. Nightmare had to have her princess, though, and it had to have its princes. More than our hearts were at stake. More than the beings who dwelled in this imaginary land that was all that more real. Humans couldn't survive without the dreams they created.

Whatever was erasing the realms was threatening more than the woman I loved and the place I came from. I needed to talk to Dio, somehow make him see some sort of reason without getting killed in the process. There was no way Ember would accept a prince that had destroyed someone she loved.

Those thoughts occupied me as I left Dream Palace. I must have been here before when I was first created because the layout was familiar to me. Even the randomly shifting parts of the palace, and the rooms that were larger on the inside than you might expect from looking at them, not to mention the secret passages. There were so many *secret* passages that the servants used the less hidden ones as ways to get around.

I'd always been curious about Dream and Nightmare, but I'd also always assumed I'd be back here one day when the princes came to get Ember, so I hadn't thought too hard about it.

We were supposed to have an audience with the king and queen and the Dream princesses once Ember woke. I'd been curious to meet them, and I supposed I still would, but I'd likely miss seeing Ember's first meeting with the rulers. I'd been with her for so many of her first experiences, and I hadn't realized how important that was to me.

I left the palace out a side door and went into the gardens. Nic had talked one of the palace horses into carrying me. All the horses in Dream were highly intelligent—fueled by children's dreams, no doubt—and some even had special powers like teleportation and telepathy.

The gardens, which I didn't remember, gave me pause. Ember would want to spend hours here, sketching and taking in the unreal beauty of the place. If I'd had more time, I would have investigated the rows of colorful blooms and exotic plants. I spotted a couple of people napping in hammocks in what looked like a poppy field.

The stables rivaled the palace for opulent color and accommodations. I went inside and had to take a minute to stare and absorb it all. The horses who lived here lived better than royalty. The floors were soft under my feet, as if designed to cushion hooves. The air smelled of sweet hay and fresh shavings and the unmistakable aroma of equine. Even for someone as unused to being around horses as I was, I could tell this was a dream, possibly even molded by the horses themselves.

Fresh hay filled every feeder and none of the stalls had doors. Each stall had water flowing from the wall down rocks and into pools that smelled so fresh I was sure it tasted better than anything I'd ever had in the conscious realm. To top it off, most of the stalls had bowl couches sturdy enough for horses to sleep on. Each stall opened into the greenest pasture I'd ever seen.

There were stands in front of the stalls and some of them held saddles and bridles that looked especially fine, though occasionally a brightly colored saddle fit for a carousel horse replaced the more standard brown and black leather.

Most of the horses were out grazing, but a few slept on their couches. I was supposed to meet the horse that had agreed to take me here.

When I went into the center of the circular building, a red horse with a metallic sheen to his coat waited for me. I didn't know a lot about horses, but this one had a big, bold head and a friendly expression.

"His name is Bug."

I turned. A woman with a long braid and a friendly smile walked up to me.

"Do you require a saddle?" she asked.

"Uh. I guess it's up to him. The only horse I've ever ridden was one of those white ones, and they didn't use saddles."

She nodded. "You'll want one, then."

I went over to the horse and rubbed his nose while I waited for her to get him ready for me.

"Thank you."

He nodded his big head and leaned into my scratches.

It didn't take long for the woman to get Bug ready to go. He followed us out of the stable and the woman helped me mount.

"All right. Let's find Dio."

The horse nodded his head.

"Do you need anything to track him down?"

Bug shook his head and headed out into the city. Letting the horse do all the navigating, I gawked.

The city surrounding Dream Palace was a bizarre mashup of a fantasy novel combined with modern-day cities, except the city portion had flying cars and trains. The road I traveled down divided the two halves. The fantasy novel half of the city was full of delicious scents, beings selling their wares, winged fairies flying about, people riding horses, dinosaurs, even a few cows. Animals were everywhere amongst the people. I saw beings flitting around from rooftop to rooftop dressed in capes and doing crazy dives off high places, landing unscathed in unlikely piles of straw. Guards occasionally dealt with the random pick pocket or other scoundrel type of character but didn't seem to imprison anyone. At least as far as I could tell in the time I had to watch.

On the city side, flying cars dodged around long trains hanging from tracks suspended in the sky. Beings hurried along sidewalks, clutching steaming cups of coffee and homey coffee shops showed on every street corner. Fancy shops mingled with people selling antiques and crafts, and a farmer's market had sprung up along one road. Musicians played everywhere, some better than others.

I saw some beings cross back and forth between the two areas, but most seemed content in whatever area they'd been dreamed up in. It was a chaotic mix that felt both harmonious and discordant.

Grateful that Bug navigated while I gawked, I patted his neck and kept glancing back and forth. At some point, I really wanted to explore.

It made me wonder what Nightmare had been like before not-Baz had begun his systematic destruction of the realm. And why? What was his goal? That question had been nagging at me for a while, but so far we didn't have many answers, just speculation.

We finally made it out of the city and into the wilds that surrounded it. I suspected, like many of the rooms in Dream Palace, both sides of the city were bigger than they looked from the outside, with many places and different cultures for dreamers to adventure.

Bug tossed his head before increasing his speed. I hung on and hoped I wasn't bouncing on his back too much. It wouldn't take much for the horse to decide he was done with my incompetent riding and toss me. I rocked my hips with his motion and tried to settle in.

Dakota Brown

CHAPTER 22

Dio

And I was stuck. Damn it.

I didn't have the energy to shift back, but I didn't want to remain in my feline shape any longer.

Hissing and swatting at a nearby tree, I yowled in frustration as the damn tree dodged my swipe. It swung a branch at me, which I didn't evade in time, and my wings didn't have the strength to hold me in the air.

I really need to figure out how to get my energy back, I thought as I picked myself up out of the dirt and licked at my shoulder. Everything hurt from the fall, and I wanted to curl up in a ball and sleep until it was all over.

Maybe I needed a good nap.

I prowled amongst the trees until I found one that wasn't likely to dodge my claws and wearily launched myself at the trunk. Digging my claws in slowed the fall as gravity took hold, and my tired limbs couldn't keep up. This time when I tumbled to the ground, I stayed there, panting.

"Aww, is the poor putty tat tired?" a voice cooed.

Lifting my head to see who was talking took a monumental effort. Oddly, a woman wearing an evening gown from an era well before Ember's stood there. A couple of dream beings waited behind her. If I had to guess, they were vampires from either the edges of Nightmare, or the boundary lands.

"I heard a rumor you were having a hard time coming back from your separation. I guess it's right. Grab him." She gestured vaguely in my direction before turning away.

Yowling, I struck out with claws and teeth, the acrid bite of vampire blood a bitter counterpoint to my defeat as they overpowered me. Me! A prince of Nightmare overpowered by mere vampires. *Fuck.*

I now bore the indignity of being stuffed in a large sack and slung over someone's shoulder. I shouldn't have even fit in the bag, but dream logic was clearly at play here. I'd tried to claw through the material, but whatever it was made of, they'd planned on keeping a clawed being contained. I spent a few precious moments and much of my remaining energy attempting to shift. That also failed, so finally I curled up and tried to rest.

Some indeterminate time later, one of the vampires dragged me out by the scruff of the neck. I thought about hissing and taking a swipe at them, but what was the point? They'd clearly won.

"Feeling a little defeated?" The woman grinned. "You'll make a lovely rug once we've drained your essence."

I snarled.

She laughed.

Fuck, that's why I'd done it in the first place. People had come after my essence. They'd already gotten Baz's. I'd hid mine, but I hadn't had time to warn Nic. Mr. Shadows was so slippery, I hadn't been nearly as worried about him getting caught.

Sighing, I didn't bother to fight as they tied my paws together, strapped my wings down painfully, and hung me from a tree. We hadn't gone too far. We were still in the Wandering Forest—named both for the trees that were far more mobile than they should be, and the movable nature of the woods itself. It wasn't always easy to find.

Hanging from my front legs was painful, but that was nothing compared to knowing I'd never see Ember—even from a distance—again.

Hot fire pulled a scream from my muzzle as they jabbed something into my skin, probably a knife, and ripped down my stomach.

I couldn't help thrashing, trying to get away, but I was stuck and so totally fucked.

Someone shouted, and I wasn't sure what happened next, but suddenly I was falling. I landed hard, twisting a joint in my back legs as I hit.

One of the vampires ran past, flinging dirt in my face. Whatever had gone after them, it gave me a minute to chew the ropes around my front paws. I almost had them undone when the damn knight fell to his knees next to me and sliced through the rest of my bonds, starting with my back paws. The rope around my midsection that trapped my wings to my sides hurt like a bitch when he pulled it away from my skin so he could get his knife underneath.

I hissed a warning, and Geraint dodged a strike from one of the vampires just in time. He turned, lunging upward with the knife he held and plunging it into the dream creature's chest.

The vampire screamed, flinging the knight away. The creature scrambled to his feet, creating a sword out of the essence flowing around us. Obviously, this vampire had been born in one part of Dream or another. Vampires created in the conscious realm couldn't use the essence like this one could.

Geraint scrambled to his feet, but he wasn't fast enough. The vampire slid his sword into the knight's chest. Geraint's eyes went wide, and he dropped his sword, collapsing.

I took the moment of distraction and launched myself onto the vampire's back. I clamped down on the creature's neck, trying not to get too much blood in my mouth, but pulling hard at his essence. After a sluggish start, the energy flowed into me as was my right as a prince. The vampire jerked his sword free of the knight, making a feeble swing at me, but it was too late. He disintegrated, and I fell, landing on top of Ember's knight.

Not wanting Ember to deal with the pain of losing someone she so obviously loved, I pushed some of my essence into the knight. Not that I had much to spare. What I'd stolen from the vampire—the irony of that was not lost on me—was only enough to heal the wound he'd given me.

I hissed angrily as the energy failed to heal the knight.

He coughed. "S'okay," he slurred. "Tell Ember I love her."

"What the fuck, Dio!"

I twisted, looking over my shoulder. Ember swirled out of the shadows and ran toward me, rage contorting her features.

Still unable to shift back, I jumped off the knight, hoping she could help him. Still glaring at me, she fell to her knees next to her lover and put her hands on his chest. I could feel his energy strengthen.

Not wanting to watch their reunion, and not able to do anything to help, I scampered away into the woods. I was glad she'd arrived in time to save her knight, and I was grateful he'd arrived in time to save me.

"I'm going to kill him," was the last thing I heard Ember say before I trotted out of hearing range.

I didn't get far before the question of who she wanted to kill was answered. Shadows writhed from the black areas between light and snapped around me tightly before jerking me up in the air.

Ember swirled out of shadow once more, looking like a goddess of vengeance, her hair flying wildly, her clothing a skintight black unitard. She stalked forward, squeezing the shadows around me.

"What were you thinking? Why? He came after you to make sure you were safe, and you did that?" She pointed back in the direction I'd come in.

Shit, she thinks I hurt her knight. I tried, one last time, to shift.

I managed it, barely, then hung limp in her shadowy grip.

"I get you don't want to share me with him but killing him isn't going to make me want you."

"Ember!"

Geraint, panting, crashed through the underbrush.

"What!" she snapped. Her fury almost made the air crackle around us.

No... there were sparks. She was truly coming into some of her powers if she were able to unconsciously affect the world around us like that.

I tried to protest, but the tendril she'd had around my throat tightened. Digging my fingers into the shadow, and knowing from years dealing with Nic that it wouldn't do any good, I clawed at it, trying to get a breath.

"Ember, let him go. He didn't hurt me."

She turned away from me. "What? Yes, he did. I saw—"

"Not what you think. Let him go, I'll explain," Geraint gasped, still clutching his midsection. Probably not as healed as he ought to be.

She let go of the shadows, and I found myself crashing to the ground yet again.

"Geraint, you should be resting."

"You should not be trying to kill Dio. Or anyone. You're not a killer, Ember." Geraint sank to the ground, sitting on a downed log. She went to her knees and funneled more energy into him.

"That woman we saw in the forgotten dream and a few vampires had Dio trapped. I cut him loose, but the vampire got me. He got the vampire and was trying to save me when you showed up." The knight put his hand on Ember's shoulder.

I rolled to my hands and knees before rubbing at my throat.

Ember glanced over at me, but she didn't look particularly sorry with narrowed eyes and gray shadows still swirling around her.

"Why are you two after me?" My voice sounded terrible after she'd nearly crushed my throat.

"We wanted to make sure you were safe," Geraint said.

"Well, I am." I struggled to my feet. "Now go back to Dream Palace and leave me alone."

They let me leave. The last part of me that had hoped Ember still wanted me shriveled up and died. At least her knight was here to make sure she got back to the others safely. Hell, she had Nic's powers. She'd probably have to make sure he got back to the palace in one piece.

A wave of dizziness washed over me. I considered going back and asking Ember to heal me like she had her knight. No, I'd get back home and see if that did it. Surely being in the darker dream energies would fully connect me to my essence.

She didn't want me, and I'd have to do without her. My love for Ember and my desire to keep her for always could join the other forgotten dreams, crumbling away on the edges of our realm until no one was left to remember what had sparked the dream in the first place.

CHAPTER 23

Ember

"Geraint, what do I do?"

My knight wrapped me in his arms and held me close. "Go after Dio, but maybe don't attack him this time."

"Why? If he wants to be left alone, and he won't budge on anything, what's the point?" I curled into his embrace, feeling guilty and pissed off that I felt uncomfortable.

"If nothing else, we need to make sure that woman doesn't get a hold of him again. He's weak. I think he needs you to pull him fully back together."

"I offered already. He said no."

"He's hurt and confused. Go after him. I'll hang back and do my best to watch for anything that might try to eat us." Geraint said the last with a smile, but we were close to Nightmare, and that was a genuine concern.

I didn't have the energy for another trip through shadow. My skills had improved drastically, but that didn't mean it was easy. So, I'd have to go after Dio the old-fashioned way.

Setting off in the direction the prince had gone in, I tried to quiet my footsteps and sneak up on him. He liked games of chase, especially when he was the hunter. I'd always been his favorite prey. Well, now he could be the hunted, at least for a while.

I hadn't been good at stalking quietly through the forest as a kid, though I was better at it than I was now. Wincing as a branch snapped under my foot, I hurried forward and hoped I wouldn't lose him. He was much better at tracking than I was, too. I could probably find him with the shadows, but I wasn't very good at that, yet.

"Go back to Dream Palace where it's safe," Dio called.

I shifted my direction, using his voice as a beacon.

"Dio, you need to come with us."

"I need to get back to Nightmare," he replied, his voice coming from a slightly different direction.

"You need to let me help you," I said more quietly.

He didn't reply, so either he hadn't heard, or he didn't want to acknowledge what I'd said.

Trying to stretch out my senses through the shadows that lurked everywhere in this forest, I attempted to track Dio that way. I caught a glimpse and picked up my pace to a jog.

An arm snaked out and wrapped around my waist, grabbing me before I could tumble down a ravine I hadn't seen.

"Caught you this time," he said, pulling me close.

"This time?"

"You don't remember crashing down into that deep ravine when we were kids? Nic caught you almost at the bottom. Lucky shadow boy was around." Dio's familiar accent and comforting arms conflicted sharply with the distance he'd kept from me, as if now that he held me, he couldn't let me go.

"Oh, uh, I'd forgotten. I think that's where my fear of falling came from now that you mention it." I relaxed into his embrace, letting him lead me back from the edge a few steps.

"Probably. You never thought twice about heights before that." He inhaled deeply. "You smell so good."

"Like sweat?" I wrinkled my nose.

His breath tickled my hair. "No, like you. Where's your knight?"

"He's around. Keeping watch."

"I can't share you with someone who is not my brother," Dio said.

I took a breath and pushed away. "Dio, let's just do whatever it is we have to do to help Nightmare and you. You don't have to share, but I'm not giving him up."

"I'm not finished," he said.

I snapped my mouth shut and glared.

"Princess, I can't share with anyone who isn't my brother, but I'd call Geraint brother if he would let me. He protected you when we could not. He didn't take you as a lover until years after we should have come back into your life. He saved me when he could have simply watched me die, and Nic told me he was prepared to die for you on more than one occasion. A man like that is certainly worthy of your love, and he's more than proven his loyalty. If he'll let me, I'd like a chance to prove I'm worthy of his friendship."

Dio stared over my shoulder. I guessed Geraint stood back there, watching. I couldn't believe what I was hearing, but if that made it possible for Dio to accept my knight, I was all for it.

I glanced over my shoulder, still in Dio's arms.

Geraint leaned against a tree, arms crossed. He studied both of us before he nodded. "Of course, your highness."

Dio shook his head. "No titles." He loosened his grip on my arms and when I stepped back, he went over to Geraint. "I would have you call me Dio, or whatever you prefer."

Geraint bowed his head slightly, then held out his hand. Dio took it without hesitation.

"Then, brother, I suggest you spend some time with Ember before we go back. See if you can work things out. I'll keep watch."

Dio smiled. "I do need to go to Nightmare before we return to Dream Palace, but we're not far from the border. I don't think a visit will take long."

"That should be fine. I think we're relatively alone, though I admit I'm a bit out of my element." Geraint glanced around himself as if to illustrate.

I shut my eyes and reached out with my shadow senses. "Wildlife, but nothing that seems interested in us," I said. "At least, as far as I can tell with my powers. I'm not very good with them yet."

"Good enough to drag someone else through shadow more than once. Even Nic can't do that," Dio pointed out.

"Yeah, it kind of sucked for everyone though," I said.

"Let's practice sometime when lives aren't actually at stake. Maybe we can make it better." Dio traded a last look with Geraint before my knight went back into the woods to keep watch.

Dio turned his attention back to me. "I'm sorry my leaving put Geraint in danger."

"It put you in danger, too."

"And if you had come after me instead of your knight, I would have put you in danger instead. I shouldn't have left." He took a breath. "I doubt I'd make a different decision if I went back and did it again, but I am sorry."

"That woman is a dreambound, and she wants to destroy the realm because she thinks it will allow her to return home. She's not going to stop until she's annihilated everything."

"She's the cause of all of this?" Dio raised his eyebrows.

"I think so, yes."

"We need to let the others know."

"We need to figure out what's wrong with Baz, too. It's going to take all of us to stop her, I think."

Dio nodded, his curls falling into his face. He brushed them away. "I think they stole his essence. If I'm remembering correctly, I fled to the conscious realm and separated from mine to avoid them getting a hold of it."

"Yeah, what was up with that creepy cornfield place?" I shuddered.

"The fields would have consumed anyone who crossed with ill intent. I set it up before I broke myself in half."

"Can you get rid of the corn?"

Dio shook his head. "Once the corn is summoned, it remains."

Why are cornfields so freaking creepy? I rubbed goosebumps that rose on my arms.

"Speaking of essence. Can you please see if you can feed me some energy? I'm sorry I refused earlier."

"Of course, Dio." The last of my residual anger fled. He was trying.

I shifted back a step from the ravine, a cool breeze with a fetid note making my skin crawl.

"Maybe we should move away from the giant rift in the ground." I stepped back.

"Yes."

I took Dio's hand, and we moved into the woods. Geraint checked in with us once to let us know he was keeping an eye on the ravine, then let us have our space. I didn't know what I'd done to deserve the knight in my life, but I sent up thanks I had him, and Nic, and it seemed now Dio.

Once we were far enough away that we felt safe, I reached up and put my hands on Dio's chest. His energy was weak, but it responded to me, curling around my fingers like a cat rubbing on someone's leg.

"How come I didn't know you were also a winged cat?" I grinned up at him.

"We obviously couldn't tell you." He grinned. "Although I had always wished we could. I almost did a few times, but we were already breaking so many rules."

"Well, I got shadow powers from Nic. What will I get from you?"

Dio tilted his head. "Are we going to have sex, then?"

I smoothed my hand over his cheek. "If you want to. I assumed that was where we were headed."

The prince took my hands in his. "Only if you want it, Ember."

"Let's see how we feel after I do this." I remembered what it had been like with Nic. Each time we'd shared energy, the desire had gotten stronger.

My stomach was tightening in anticipation already. It could be different with Dio, but I doubted it.

I pushed tendrils of energy into him. He sucked in his breath, grabbed around my waist, and pulled me against him. His arousal heightened mine, and I was glad I was wearing dream clothing instead of my conscious realm stuff. I could shed it fast, not to mention make a blanket out of it for us to lay on.

Not wanting to rush, and needing to make sure he had all the energy he needed to become whole, I kept my clothing firmly in place.

Energy flowed between us as I poured more into my wounded prince. I felt the weak spots in the flow of his own energy and tried to direct the essence to fill it up and repair the tears he'd made when he separated himself.

I wasn't sure how long I worked on him, but finally it was as if everything clicked into place and Dio became as whole as I could make him.

He groaned, fingers digging into my back, and his erection pressing into my front. I tilted my head back and met his eyes.

"Thank you, princess." His voice was breathless, and he trembled. "I don't know that I've ever felt a need like this."

"Kiss me, Dio."

He met my lips with his, gently at first, as if amazed he was actually kissing me. He grew confident after a few gentle presses of his lips. Dio's hands moved to cup my ass, and I threaded my fingers through his curls.

"You're amazing, princess," he breathed between kisses. "I'm so grateful Nic convinced Mary to take us through that arch all those years ago."

"Mmm, me too," I murmured. "Never expected anything like this, but I certainly don't want to give it up."

Dio's hands slid up under my shirt and kneaded my back.

"So, we're both wearing dream clothing," I said, "and we need a blanket."

He grinned at me as I let my clothing melt into a puddle at my feet, then commanded it to spread out into a blanket. After a quick hesitation, Dio's joined mine, and I got my first look at my primal prince. Lean, with long, powerful, cat-like muscles, a delicious V that led down to—

"Dio?"

"Ahh, um, barbed for your pleasure." He winked. "Also, I believe there may be some locking involved."

"Uh."

"Feline, remember. I think you'll like it. Unlike real cats, this shouldn't actually hurt you."

"Oh." I paused. "Oh! Shit, yeah, let's do this."

He chuckled at my enthusiasm. "I wish to explore you, my princess, before you get impaled on my cock and can't get away."

"I don't want to get away."

"Good." He gently lowered me to the ground. "I'm going to take you from behind, and I'm going to mark you, and there will be no question to anyone that you are mine."

"Mark me?"

"Mmm, yes, my teeth in your shoulder. Might hurt, will heal quickly when we share our essence. It will leave a mark."

"All right," I agreed. "Nic didn't mark me."

"Oh, he did, just not with his teeth. Anyone who can see or sense essence can feel his shadows around you all the time. It's subtle, just like him."

Knowing that I already bore Nic's mark, and that I would soon have Dio's warmed me. It felt right, like I would be a little more complete. Maybe Geraint and I could come up with something for us, so I could have a mark from all of them.

"But first, I want you screaming my name." He walked around me, inspecting his prize.

Dio ran his fingers lightly over the harlequin silks tattoo I had on my shoulder, reminding me of when Geraint, Ash, and I had gotten them together. Maybe I already did have his mark.

"Fitting," he whispered, before placing his lips on my skin, then continuing his circle around me. "You are incredibly beautiful. Powerful. A worthy mate." He said the last with a wink when he met my eyes. "I shall do my best to also be worthy."

I stepped forward, a hand going to his chest, the other to his hip, pulling Dio against me as I kissed him. I needed to taste him, to consume him, to feel the essence flowing between us.

214

He pressed his tongue to mine, exploring my mouth, letting me explore his. As we kissed, his hands roamed my body, kneading my back, fingers digging into my ass, lifting me off my feet until he could guide us both to the ground. The blanket we'd crafted cushioned my back so I couldn't feel the branches or rocks or other irregularities in the earth.

The cool Nightmare air caressed my skin as if claiming me, just like Dio was claiming me. A flock of ravens cawed in the distance, and I imagined they approved of their queen getting taken by their feline prince in their forest.

Dio trailed his kisses along my jaw, until he could nip me gently behind my ear. I arched up into him, wanting to be filled.

"Patience," he murmured. "You've got some screaming to do first."

Whatever I might have said was cut off by a sharper nip at the base of my throat. I cried out, digging nails into his skin.

"Mmm, yes, draw blood if you want," he said, biting down again before cautioning me. "Tell me if I'm too rough."

"I will."

He gently explored my breasts, kneading, rolling my nipples between his fingers before sucking one into his mouth then blowing across it.

I whimpered, tilting my hips, wanting his touches, and wanting more at the same time.

He nipped me again, as if chastising me for my impatience before continuing his slow, torturous, but delightful exploration of my body until finally, finally, he reached my pussy. His study of my soaked folds was tentative at first, but he gained confidence as he discovered my clit.

"Dio, yes, that!" I cried out as he sucked the sensitive nub. "Fuck, yes."

He added a finger into the mix, sliding it inside me and curling it.

"There," I said when he found my g-spot.

Dio took my directions well and twitched his finger, trying different motions until he had me squirming.

"I'm so close, Dio." I lifted my hips, wanting more. Needing more.

"Come now, princess," he murmured before returning his attention to my clit.

I shattered, shouting his name.

"Very good," he whispered in my ear. "In the future, you'll scream my name a few more times, but right now I don't want to wait. I want you."

"Then take me, Dio. Claim me. Mark me. Bind me."

"I intend to."

He rolled me over until my ass was in the air, his hands on my hips.

"I've wanted you for so long," he said with a hitch in his lust-filled voice.

"You have me."

Dio thrust into me, his unique cock with its ridges and barbs stimulating me in new and fascinating ways. I shoved back into him, and my eyes widened as Dio purred.

"Fuck me," I breathed. I felt his purring all the way into my core. All of him was vibrating, and I did mean all of him.

"I am," he said with a quiet laugh.

I was quickly beyond thinking as Dio pounded into me, his cock swelling, the barbs pressing out enough to rub me on the inside, but not enough to cause pain.

My legs trembled, and I was so close to coming again that I nearly cried when he slowed.

"Dio!"

"You need a mark before you shatter on my cock." He leaned forward and sank his teeth into my shoulder, the opposite one that had my tattoo.

I yelled, partially in pain, partially in pleasure. My body came apart, orgasm ripping through me.

Dio grunted his own release, shuddering into me. He licked the wound on my neck then eased us both down onto our sides, still bound together by his swollen cock.

We lay there for a bit, floating in our endorphin-induced haze and enjoying each other's arms.

"See? A little different than real cats," he murmured after a while. "They don't get to enjoy being stuck together, either."

"Too bad for them."

"They don't get this, either."

When he slid out of me, my body shattered again from the rub of his barbs inside me.

"That's a hell of a perk," I managed to get out.

He kissed my cheek. "Having you is the best perk."

Dakota Brown

CHAPTER 24

Ember

I hadn't felt this good in weeks. A great deal of worry had eased from my mind. We knew where Baz was, and he was relatively safe. Dio was mine, Nic and Geraint were mine, and we knew what was going on with the attempt to destroy the Dream realms. While we didn't know how to stop it, we were quite a bit closer to that goal.

Dio and I walked hand in hand as we traveled deeper into Nightmare. I wasn't sure if it was because of my increased connections with Dio and Nic, and my practice with my shadow powers, or something else, but I could tell the instant we crossed from the boundary lands into Nightmare. It felt like coming home.

Despite the danger of the realm, tension eased from my shoulders and the muscles around my neck loosened.

Dio took a deep breath. "It feels good to be home."

"Yeah." My thoughts turned toward Ash and Casey and my joy faltered.

"What's wrong, dearest?" Dio stopped and looked at me. Geraint touched my shoulder.

"I'm worried about Ash and Casey."

"If your jester friend is half as honorable as he seems, he will make sure Casey adjusts well to her new home. Ash, well, I suppose we'll have to take care of her."

"Dio, Ash is engaged. She's supposed to get married in a couple of months. They were talking about having a baby." I fought off tears.

Dio wrapped his arms around me. "It's done, Ember, and I don't know any way to fix it, but we'll try."

"Thanks." I let him comfort me, let him make me think everything would be okay.

"How is she doing?" Dio squeezed me tight before letting go.

"Actually, she acts fine, but she's good at hiding her feelings when she wants too, so I don't actually know."

"Let's focus on the most immediate problems first. Then we'll see what we can do for Ash. We've got to wake up Baz before we can do much else." Dio kissed my forehead.

"You're right. And right now I'm going to enjoy being back in Nightmare, as strange as it feels to say that."

"Speaking of." Dio grinned at me before dropping to his knees.

I watched in fascination as he melded into the winged panther. It wasn't like a movie werewolf's transformation, but more of a melting from Dio the man, to Dio the feline.

He stretched his wings, flapping them as if testing their strength. My feline prince tucked his wings tight against his body before rubbing against my legs. His shoulders came up to my hips in this shape. I thought he was a little bigger than he had been before I'd helped heal him. After nearly pushing me over with his affectionate rubbing, he turned his attention to Geraint.

Feeling like I could probably get away with it, I let my fingers run over Dio's back as he walked away from me and shoved his head against my knight's hip. Geraint smiled and hesitantly pet Dio's head. The prince pushed into Geraint's touch, cat-like.

Guess he was serious about the brother thing.

After Dio spent a few minutes twining around the two of us, he bounded off, stretched his wings, and gave a mighty leap. His wings caught the air, and he soared.

I put my hand over my mouth, gasping at the sheer joy and beauty of my prince flying.

"So, what do you think you'll get from Dio?" Geraint winked at me, coming over and putting his arm around my waist. He'd been hesitant to touch me, despite Dio's assurances that he had accepted Geraint.

I leaned into my knight's familiar embrace.

"Well, Nic's got cool shadowy powers. I don't actually know what powers Dio has, other than shape shifting and flying."

"He's certainly got some form of heightened senses. He smelled my scent all over you before he was even really conscious again."

"Huh, maybe that's why I'm thinking you need to take a shower," I playfully nudged Geraint's side.

He laughed. "We both need a shower." Geraint squeezed me against him and kissed my head. We watched while Dio soared above us.

After a time, Dio turned and looked behind us. He hovered, as if watching before he dove.

The urgency in Dio's flight got my heart racing. I glanced over my shoulder, but all I could see were trees.

He landed in front of us, hitting the ground hard and skidding a little before he melted back into his human shape.

"Nothingness storm. We need to run!" He pointed deeper into Nightmare. "Ember, if you can shadow walk, do it now. Get back."

The urgency in Dio's voice quelled my protest. I reached for the shadows, but they slipped through my fingers, and pain shot through my temples.

"I'm still recovering from the last one," I said.

"This way." Dio ran farther into Nightmare, and we followed.

Before long we broke out of the trees and into an open field. Familiar white puffy clouds flitted around in the gray sky. Small, light colored objects fell from the clouds.

I was so focused on the clouds and what they were doing, that I didn't notice what stretched ahead of us.

"Shit." Dio skidded to a halt.

I brought my attention down. Corn. Massively tall stalks of corn blocked our progress and the field spread for miles in either direction. The corn was starkly green against the prevalent grays and whites and blacks of Nightmare. It didn't seem to have any shades, similar to many other things in Nightmare.

Above, creatures flitted about as if trying to catch whatever the clouds were dropping. Where the flying creatures missed, the corn rustled as the objects went into the depths.

"What are those?" I breathed, pointing.

I could see the exact moment when the clouds and the other creatures noticed the nothingness storm. They all froze their movement and hovered, before speeding away faster than I could keep track of.

"Those were tooth fairies. They were gathering teeth from the young clouds who were teething."

"That's fucking horrifying," Geraint replied.

"What's worse is we're going to die if Ember can't transport us." Dio scanned the horizon as if looking for another solution.

We turned. The gray smear of the nothingness bore down on us.

The corn rustled behind us.

I whimpered and reached for the shadows, but like before, they slipped through my fingers. "I can't. Not yet." Desperately, I tried to create a storm shelter like I had ages ago. I'd felt good not long ago, but certainly not rested after several trips through the shadows, taking others with me. My powers resisted my attempts to manipulate the world around me. Tears sprang to my eyes as I tried again.

Dio swore as we watched our destruction speed toward us.

"We have to go into the corn," I whispered, ashamed of my failure.

Dio blanched, and Geraint gripped my hand.

"Dio." I took his hand when he didn't answer. "We *have* to go into the corn."

He shuddered, but we were out of time. I couldn't save us, so we had to risk the fields that even the twins and the tooth fairies wouldn't enter. I wondered what we would find if we could outrun the storm.

Holding both Geraint and Dio's hands, I turned, pulling them with me, and ran into the corn.

The End

Stay tuned for the third and final book in the Dreambound trilogy, Nightmare's Flight

Author's Note

Thank you so much for reading my reverse harem tale! More is coming soon! Reviews are so very important, especially to new authors and are greatly appreciated! Even a line or two will do!

About the Author

Dakota has two passions in life: writing and cinnamon tea. Tea so strong she ought to be able to see her future when she drinks it, and the writing? Well, she hopes it makes you see stars when you read it. She creates reverse harem romance novels filled with things that go bump in the night. That handsome werewolf walking down the street? The suave vampire you're just dying to get a taste of? You'll find them enraptured by charming, smart ladies ready to make those bad boys work for their affection. When not writing, Dakota can be found on the back of a horse out on the trail or tending the animals on her farm.

Other Works

Mountain Magic Trilogy (complete)

Becoming
Demon's Touch
Reckoning

Ocean Enchantment Trilogy

Siren's Catch
Siren's Song
Siren's Storm

Pizza Shop Exorcist (complete)

The Price of Possession
The Price of Exorcism
The Price of Magic
The Price of Souls
The Price of Rebellion

Horsemen Against the Apocalypse Duet

Seeking War
Apocalypse Interrupted

Dreambound Trilogy

Nightmare's Dance
Nightmare's Fall
Nightmare's Flight